Sin on a Dark Knight

SINS
BOOK ONE

RHIANNON FUTCH

To all the bitches.
You are amazing.
Keep changing, growing, and
never settle for less than you deserve.

Contents

$$One$$

JASMINE

PUTTING the key in the ignition, I wish, for the
thousandth time, that I had a car new enough to have a
keyless ignition, and that I didn't have to pray to the old
gods would start. Muttering, "Here goes nothing," I turn
the key. I immediately worry that I used up the end of my
luck for today when it fires right up. Easing her into drive, I
pull out of my spot in the Southern House parking lot and
immediately stop when I remember I haven't sorted the
money yet. Reversing back into that same spot, I put her in
park and pull the wad of money from my apron. Three
hundred dollars tonight. I did great, much better than I
thought I had. I quickly count out a hundred in the
smallest bills, so it stays a larger wad that he won't suspect
has been skimmed. The other two hundred I stuff in my
purse. I'll swing by the atm and deposit that tonight. Best if
it stays in the bank where there's no chance he'll see it.

The bank is near to my job, thankfully. Waiting tables is

not the easiest or most fun job, but it pays the bills if you work it right and gives you some to save for running away if you work it better. I get to the ATM and slip my card out of the secret pocket in the red bag in my purse, looking around because I am always worried he has gotten a ride to come follow me around. The last time he did, I spotted them before I ever got out of the restaurant. I never trust that he hasn't gotten sneakier since then because he said he knew I had seen him and that I would never see him coming next time he checked up on me.

I finish my deposit, still scanning the area around me for cars or people out of place. Thank fuck he is more brawn than brains or I would be in trouble. I don't even begin to relax my vigilance until I am far from the bank. I have five thousand squirreled away in that account, but I know if he beat me hard enough, I would get it out for him or write him a check like I did last time. This is not the first time I have tried to save up enough to get away from him. It is the last time.

This time he won't find my bank statement and come beat me till I give him the money so he can try making another investment. Everything being electronic means I have everything connected to an email hidden deep in my phone. By investment, he means buy a bunch of drugs to sell. Which, admittedly, could make money. If he didn't do the drugs with his stupid friends. I hate him, but he is vicious and getting away from him is going to be expensive. So here I am, two thousand from my goal, and on my way home to another night of the worst sex I have ever had and whatever he berates me for today.

The lights of the city zip by as I head for the trailer park on the outskirts. I would never have gone with him all those years ago if he hadn't been so damn charming. And if I hadn't been living in my aunt's place. That place was even worse than how he is now. She kept trying to sell me, but I am vicious when I fight and I refused to be her whore. Then Fabio came into my life. He was hot back then, and so charming. I was swept off my feet; stupid, young, naïve me. His charm didn't last half as long as our marriage has and now I have been trying to leave him for the past five years, without success.

Turning into the shared driveway of the trailer park, I see some strange people milling about in small groups, but whatever, probably another party. Maybe he will be at the party and I can get some sleep while he's gone. Fingers crossed, I pull up to our trailer. The sun should come up in another twenty minutes or so. Maybe I can watch the sunrise from the kitchen if he is still partying.

I tuck my purse away in the trunk by opening the middle console of the back seat. Closing it, I turn around and take a deep breath. I lock my door as I get out, knowing that I keep the rest of them locked always, I don't even need to check them. I hear some guys catcalling me, but I ignore them and head for the steps to get to the trailer. We have a small wooden porch attached to the front door of the trailer; the trailer being raised to avoid possible flooding. I get up the stairs and I hear my cat caller yell, "Lady, you don't wanna go in there. Much nicer here, I'll keep you safe!" Probably would have been more reassuring if he hadn't ended that on a maniacal laugh. It appears he met Fabio, though, and is just as impressed with him as I am. I open the door with a twist and a snatch. It always sticks. I hear maniacal laughter guy shouting again, "Don't say I didn't warn you!"

Reaching in, I hit the light switch next to the door and yelp. Blood. Blood everywhere. My breathing is short gasps as I turn and stumble back down the stairs. Backing away from the porch, I hear a different voice. This one sounds dangerous in a way the manic laugher guy didn't as he says, "Aw, you don't like our little surprise?"

Spinning around, shock is replaced with the acute awareness provided by an adrenalin rush. "I won't tell. I will turn around and leave. No one will ever see me again. You won't have to worry about me, I promise."

He steps out of the shadow of one of the trees, giving me my first look at him. He is gorgeous. Why are the bad ones always gorgeous? He is tall, dark, and handsome, the light from the full moon glinting off his skin. His dark hair is long and mussed, but it just makes him hotter. He sniffs the air and smiles, saying, "I love it when the adrenaline hits the blood. It smells like such a high. Are you scared, sweetheart?"

Nothing about his smile eases my mind, but I think in a different setting I could come if he read the newspaper out loud to me. He takes a step toward me and I take a step back. Sexy or not, he is not getting anywhere near me. I scan the yard, remember the door under the porch.

"Are you going to run, little bunny? I'll catch you, you know I will. And then, then I think we will have some fun."

I look him in the eye when he says little bunny, my eyes narrowing, "What did you call me?"

He looks up at the sky and holds his hand out toward me, saying, "Little bunny, we need to wrap this up. Come on, I don't leave witnesses. But you're cute. I'll give you a choice. Join us or die."

I shout, "Fuck you," as I dip under the porch and barrel through the little door. I hear him still talking as I crawl toward the far end of the trailer. There is a loose piece of siding there that I can escape through. He figures out that I am not under the porch and I hear him singsong at the doorway, "Oh look, little bunny has run. I'm coming to find you! Ready or not, here I come!"

I crawl faster, knowing he has to crawl too and that will slow him down, plus he doesn't know which way I went. Something hits my hand and throws off my crawl. I fall face first onto... a chest?

I straighten up and whisper, "Who the hell are you? Why are you under...? Never mind, help me. There is a guy after me."

This low purr of a voice drifts up in the darkness as he says, "Darlin', I'm more dangerous than he is. You aren't upgrading here."

"Maybe not, but I still think you could help me. I just need to get back in my car and I will be gone. Please," my voice cracks, "don't let me be murdered just as I get free from him."

The man under me growls, "Fuck." I can hear him getting closer when the man under me grabs me and rolls to the right, putting me under him and kisses me. My legs spread of their own accord and he snugs himself directly between them.

He cuts off the kiss and hisses at the darkness to our left, saying, "She's mine."

I hear the other sexy voice not far off in the darkness, "I saw her first."

"I claim her," the guy on top of me said and then some strange power emanated from him, it felt like power and raw sex, my pelvis jumped up to press against his erection causing me to get a lot closer to an orgasm than I thought possible considering I was laying under the trailer my husband had been murdered in, dirt on my backside and two strange guys fighting over who gets to claim me while I dry hump one's pelvis. Yes, this is just a normal day, nothing to see here...

The guy chasing me hisses and says, "Fine. She is yours. For now. We'll see if you can keep her tonight."

I hear him move away and the guy over me presses his hardness against me, sending shivers through my body, "Makes it difficult to scare people away when you do that. Come on, we have to get out of here before the sun rises."

He keeps hold of my wrist and leads me to the very exit I was heading for. He climbs out into the soft rays of dawn, before the sun really comes up. I scramble out and head for my car. He is right next to me, his hand hovering at the base of my spine. I can feel the coolness of him through my thin shirt. I see most of the people that were hanging around on my way in have gathered around my car. Mr. Tall-deadly-dark-and-handsome is back over by his tree shadows. Ready to melt back into them at a moment's notice, I'm sure.

I realize I haven't gotten a look at my rescuer and I start to turn my head to look at him when one of the people glaring at us hisses. My eyes are drawn to the person hissing and I stumble a bit when I see fangs. Everywhere. My eyes flit to the guy that was chasing me and he smiles, showing off his own set of fangs gleaming in the combined light of the moon and impending dawn. If this guy backed them off and they all have fangs... I whip my head around to look at him. He is pale, with dark hair secured behind his head. His mouth is firmly closed, so I can't tell if he has fangs or not. He walks me all the way to the door of my car and waits while I get in. I lock the door and lean across to unlock the passenger door. He opens it as soon as it is unlocked and slides in smoothly. I barely manage to get leaned back before he is in the seat.

Closing the door, he asks, "How did you make it home? This hunk is nearly dead."

"I know, I know. I pray every time I start her that she will make it where I am going. Here goes nothing."

I stick the key in the ignition but pause when he places his hand on the dash and it glows. Not like light from the moon reflecting, but an actual glow emanating from his hand. I watch as the glow fades and he says, "Start it. It will run now."

I know my eyes must look like saucers, but I am nothing if not cool in dangerous situations. God knows I have been through enough of them. Sure enough, she starts right up and runs in a way I never knew she could. She is nearly purring. Outstanding. I put the car in reverse, and back up. I don't worry about the people milling about because fuck them. They all have fangs and obviously mean no good for me. Judging by my husband's remains splattered about the trailer, they are really sloppy eaters, too. Double fuck those people.

I get my car pointed in the right direction and throw it in drive. Checking the rearview mirror as I head down the shared driveway, it looks like everyone is gone, but I feel him still standing there in the shadows watching me. I slant a look over at the guy in the passenger seat. I have questions, but I don't know him and I kind of don't want to piss him off. He relaxed and reclined in the seat, eyes closed. But I know he isn't asleep. I watch the sun coming up as I drive. Seeing the first rays touch his face, other than a small frown, he has no reaction. I pull into the gas station up to the pumps. He looks around, saying, "You should be safe to get gas here, but you need to come to my house. They will come find you tonight as soon as the sun sets."

I put the car in park and shut it off. Looking over at him, I go for it, asking, "Are those people what I think they are?"

"If you think they are vampires, then yes."

I juggle my keys in my hand, "What are you?"

He opens the bluest eyes I have ever seen to look directly at me and smile, revealing fangs lengthening as I watched, "A different breed of vampire."

I nod, "Ok. I'm getting gas. You want anything from the store?"

He shakes his head no, saying, "You are taking this... better than most."

I chuckle, "My life has been different than most." I turn to reach through the back seat and pull open the false console. Fuck. My purse slid back a little. I crawl halfway back so I can reach in and grab my purse. I freeze as I realize I don't have to hide it here anymore. Probably. Who knows what tonight will bring? Dragging it out and slipping back down into my seat, I open my purse and rummage for the red wallet. I find it and dig out the card. I can feel the guy watching all this and I turn to him, asking, "What?"

"Why did you have that hidden? Weren't you just getting home?"

I roll my eyes, "Yes, I was. If you must know, the guy they murdered in the trailer above where I found you was my husband. He wasn't the nicest guy ever, and he didn't particularly care for me to have anything. I was planning to leave him but had to save up, so I had my purse hidden to keep him from getting my money."

"Then why do you have a wad of cash in your apron?"

"Decoy. Look, let me get gas and we can talk about this on the road." I get out and go through the motions to get the gas started pumping. I decide to fill her up, since I don't need to keep it mostly empty to keep him from suspecting I have more money than he knows about. It really takes a lot longer to fill a car up than it does to put five in and go. Eventually, the handle clicks and it stops filling. I put everything away and get myself back in the car.

As I start the car, he asks, "Do you have any sunglasses?"

"Um, yes. Do you need some sunscreen or something?" I ask as I dig through the purse.

"Sunscreen?"

"Well, you said you're a vampire. And you mentioned I would be safe today, but tonight they would be hunting me. So I deduced that the myth about sunlight and vampires is correct. Is it not?"

He raises an eyebrow, "Very good. You are correct, but I told you I am a different breed. The sunlight won't hurt me, it is just really bright in my eyes and they are more adapted to seeing at night than facing down the light of day."

I pull the glasses out and pass them over. He slips them on as I shove everything back into my purse and set it in the back floorboard. Starting the car again, I marvel at the way it just fires right up. No whiiiiirrrriiiiirrr before it catches or anything. It's wild. Leaving the parking lot of the gas station, I ask him to give me directions.

He looks around and says, "Get on 70 and head east."

I nod and drive faster now that I have some direction. "My name is Jasmine. What's yours?"

"Mikael."

"No last name?"

He shrugs, an elegant movement of his shoulders that draws my attention, "I changed it and I don't have it memorized yet. I have had a few."

"Would it be rude to ask how old you are?"

Big sigh from him, as he says, "Are you going to ask questions the whole way?"

"Yes. I worked all night. I was just getting home from that. Usually by now I am either sleeping or fighting. Talking helps me stay awake. Keeps us out of the ditch. Are there others in your breed?"

"Pull over, I can drive. I need little in the way of sleep. And the answers to your questions are 5000, give or take a few hundred and no, there is no one else quite like me."

I pull over because my eyes are really heavy and I'm a little worried. Besides, if he was going to kill me, he would have done it under the trailer. Or let the other guy have me. I hop out and run around the car to get in the passenger seat. He waits long enough for me to get the door shut before he takes off. He drives like he is in a race. His focus is insane and so is his speed.

"You know, the tires on this aren't that great. I really don't want to die in a fiery auto crash. Where do you live, anyway?"

"The far side of town. I have a big place, so I have some others living with me. Don't worry, they won't attack you on sight or anything, especially since you have my scent on you."

* * *

Leonidas

I watch her drive away. I can feel her watching me in the rearview, though I know she can't see me. Lex strolls over, "What are we gonna do 'bout her?"

Her taillights out of sight, I meet his eyes, "We are going to wait till tonight and go find her. They can't have gone far. We'll find them tonight and then we will see how tough he really is."

"Why did you stop us anyway, Leonidas? We could've took him."

I raise my brows at Lex and explain slowly, "Because he is stronger than you think, and it would've taken too long to subdue him. We would have risked frying in the sunlight. Everyone go hole up for the day. I'll be in her trailer," I say as I point it out, "meet me here tonight."

I walk away without looking to see if he does my bidding. Knowing he will because, while he isn't that smart, he has a great sense of self-preservation. I see the rays of the sun peeking over the trees and I put on the speed. Grabbing the body of her husband, I run back down the stairs and shove him through the door under the trailer. Slamming it shut, I dip back in the house just before the sun hits me. I grab the chain to pull the door closed, walking around the house closing curtains, blinds, and throwing blankets up on windows that aren't covered enough. I can smell her throughout the trailer. She smells divine. So much better than anything I have scented in years, not for lack of trying. Sadly, it would seem the criminal element I run with isn't always that able or, sometimes is less than interested in, the whole hygiene thing. Most of the women smell good. But they usually carry the scent of an unwashed man that ruins it. The man that lived here seems to have been a little more hygienic.

I'll look it all over later tonight when I wake up. Looking around, I see that the couch is relatively free from blood, so I lay down there.

Two

JASMINE

WITH HIM DRIVING, I thought I would drop right off to sleep, but no, I am wide awake and watching the scenery go by. I keep thinking I should probably be more disturbed by everything that has happened in the past hour or two. I got nothing, though. It doesn't matter that Fabio is dead. I'm not even upset that he died violently. He deserved it. He was an utter jackass the past five years, and I went to bed more than one morning wishing he were dead.

The vampire thing... I know most people would be really upset to find that we are not top of the food chain. Meh, we are really squishy to be considered the top of the food chain, in my opinion. But vampires, they live a really long time. This one can go out during the day but the rest are sun sensitive. He said he was five thousand years old. I bet he has seen some shit. The way he just backed that other guy off, that was amazing. The other guy wasn't scared, though, I don't think. I wonder what that's like? "When was the last time you were afraid of anything?"

He looks over at me, asking, "What? What do you mean?"

"I mean, when was the last time something, anything, struck fear in you? You understand the concept, right?"

His eyebrows drop as he scowls at the road ahead. "A little under five thousand years ago, when my wife disappeared."

"That long ago? So are you really strong? Was anything else enhanced when you were turned?"

"What kind of questions are these? Why — I thought you were going to sleep."

"Well, I was. But then I got to thinking about things and I had some questions. The crucial question is, what changed when you became a vampire?"

"If I answer, will you quietly think about it till we arrive at my house?"

"Yes." Probably. I watch his face twist. Maybe he isn't buying it either.

He sighs, "When I became a vampire, I became very strong. And also became allergic to sunlight for a long time. I was immediately beset with a lust for blood. Which made me become a murderer of the worst kind and subject to the fires of hell should I ever die. I am very fast and I need so little sleep at this point that I can go long periods of time with no more than a nap. My hearing, sight, taste, and sense of smell all improved exponentially. I don't need to breathe but I can't speak if I don't, physiology at work there. Plus, my sense of smell is more capable when I inhale because it brings more scents in. That is pretty much it. Now will you sleep?"

"Probably. I still have a lot of thoughts swirling in my mind right now. I might have more questions."

* * *

Mikael

She is sleeping almost as soon as she closes her eyes. She is the strangest human I have met in a very long time. I don't know exactly what to do with her. I feel like I need to protect her. There is a wildness to her that seems familiar, but I don't know why. She is nothing like my wife has ever been in any of her lives. I don't even remember the name she was married to me by anymore. She has had a dozen more names since then. I haven't been able to find her this time, though. It's almost like she hid herself from me.

Now I have this woman. She is taller than the average woman, and her skin is the color of fine porcelain. Her curly hair flows over a sumptuous body, but her eyes. Her eyes remind me of my wife. She always has those gray-green eyes that remind me of haunted moors. She doesn't feel like her, though; doesn't feel like... Emma! That was her name in the last life, Emma. She doesn't feel like Emma.

I don't understand why I had such a powerful reaction to her after she crawled over me. All the pent up sex and rage within me tried to come out right then. The way I wanted to fuck her while I killed him. I couldn't risk touching her on the way to her car. I would have killed every one of the younglings surrounding her car if I had. She nearly got a few with her car. They thought to play games, and she was unaware. Or maybe she knew. I can't read her at all. Even though I knew she was horny when I got between her legs because her hormones betrayed her, I certainly couldn't get a read on her. I should probably keep her around for a while, just to study. I should have no problems keeping my hands off her. Even if she smells fantastic.

My exit comes up and I steer to the correct lane, slowing the car. Getting off the interstate and into the city, I am minutes from home. She doesn't wake as I make the turns to get home. If she is sleeping still when I get there, then I will just carry her in. Where the hell should I put her? My bed. That is the only place no one will enter if I am not in there. They probably won't do anything to her if they find her wandering the halls, but I think I need to tell them, anyway. I pull up to the house and shut the car off after putting it in park. I can't believe she drove this thing anywhere before I worked my magic on it. The head gasket was mostly shot, the oil so burnt she may as well have been running water through the system, the spark plugs... And none of that even touches on the rods that were knocking or the filth in the transmission.

I get out of the car and stretch. It was not the most luxurious ride. I open the back door of the car and take out her purse. She had it hidden in her car. I doubt she wants it far from her. She sleeps like the dead. How is she not awake? I walk around to her door and open it. She reaches down like she is looking for a blanket to pull over her.

Fuck. I didn't really want to carry her up. After I set her purse on the hood of her car and lean in to pick her up, she snuggles into my chest as I straighten up with her. I scowl down at her, but her eyes never open and she has a little smile playing on her lips. With a kick, the door is closed and I step over to grab her purse.

I focus a moment on the front door of the house and it swings open before me, closing as I head up the stairs to my bedroom. I pass Quinn on my way down the hall. He raises an eyebrow when I growl at him, but keeps on moving. Why am I growling at him? Oh, shit. I claimed her. And when I claimed her, I really claimed her. Fuck me. No wonder I want her so damn much. I focus on my bedroom door and it opens in front of me. As I step through, I swing it closed with a foot. I walk over to my bed, looking down to nudge the sheets out of the way with my magic. Dropping her purse on the floor, I set her gently on the bed and I slip my arms from under her. While I am still leaning over her, I breathe in deeply of her scent. She smells like wild roses and earth and rain. The scents are stronger on her neck and it is there I find myself hovering. Opening my eyes to find that my teeth are just about to pierce her neck. Pushing away, I fly back from her and nearly break my dick when I try to straighten up. I crumple to the floor as it is smashed a little by my jeans. I shove a hand into my pants and rearrange it so I can stand without immense pain.

When did it get hard? Maybe I fucked up bringing her here. I don't know if I can keep my hands off her. She is just sleeping on the bed fully clothed and I want to bury my face between those glorious thighs to see if she tastes as good as she smells. Get it together, Mikael. You are stronger than a base reaction. Go cover her up and walk away. I walk over slowly, one careful step at a time. Looking down at her face, she looks so innocent in her sleep. I don't think I can make her life worse by keeping her a part of mine when she would only be a diversion until I find Emma. As I pull the sheets over her, she snuggles into the pillow. I run from the room, closing the door behind me with magic and sealing it against all others as I head for the kitchen and the sustenance I crave almost as much as I crave her.

Three

JASMINE

I OPEN my eyes to a strange room and my heart races until I remember I was with Mikael and we were heading to his house. I reach out, checking to see if there are any other bodies in the bed with me. Seems clear, so I sit up and look for a nightstand or something with a lamp on it. I find it and feel around the whole damn thing before I find the button on the base. Fucking rich people with their fancy shit. I hit the button and get a look at the lamp. It really is nice. I can't blame him. It looks like a good lamp. Fuck, do vampires drink coffee? Is that a thing I can get here? I'll have to go get some if these heathens don't have any. These sheets are really nice too. Are these silk sheets? Who cares. They feel great. This room is enormous. I see curtains on the far wall. They are pretty heavy, so I get up and wander over to see if it is evening, or I woke up early. Pulling the curtain to the side, I see humongous windows that look out onto some nicely manicured grounds. The moon is out and

I blow her a kiss. I always feel like she is watching out for me.

Turning away from the window, I check out the rest of the room. No dressers, but I see three doors, so probably one is a closet. He has a seating area over here, with two really fluffy chairs. I want to sit, but I still feel gritty from earlier and I cannot afford to pay for a cushion off this chair. With a sigh, I head back to the bed to see how dirty the sheets are from my sleeping in them.

They look good, but I swipe across them to get any dust off them, anyway. One of those doors has to be a bathroom. I need a shower, something fierce. Stripping down, I leave my clothing on the floor next to the bed. I spot my purse on the floor, too. Walking across the room, this floor feels amazing on my feet. I try the door to the right. Holy shit. This bathroom is bigger than my kitchen in the trailer. Oh Jasmine, you fell in shit and are coming up smelling roses. I wonder if this guy needs a girlfriend? No. No way do I want to be someone's girlfriend. Not even for this bathroom. The shower is across the marble room. Why does it have so many shower heads? What kind of freaky guy is he? Maybe I should check into whether he needs a temporary girl-friend. Buttons on the wall operate the shower, and it is officially the fanciest thing I have ever had my bare ass in. I figure out getting the water to turn on and it rains out of the big piece in the middle. I stick my hand under the flow and it feels like soft rain. This is a crying setting. What could he possibly have to cry about with this life? I am sure he has his reasons, but I just can't see them. I need to check these other settings. Playing with it, I get a set going that will hit my back and come down from above at a good pressure. I moan as I step into the water. It is just shy of blistering and I feel the muscles in my back easing. I stand there just letting the water hit me for a minute. Never have I been in a shower this nice and I want to enjoy it while I can. I want to live like this. Have a ridiculously luxurious shower in a bathroom bigger than my old kitchen. I didn't even realize till today that this is exactly the kind of place I want to live in. But how? Even without Fabio in the picture, I will be old before I get anywhere near this level of lux.

Unless... what if one of these people turns me? That's possible, right? I mean, the other guy was saying I had to join them or die. If they are all vamps, then it stands to reason that they can turn people. That hottie Mikael said he was around 5000 years old. That's a long time to gain the funds to this level of lux. So I just need to get someone to turn me. That should be easy and maybe I can get railed properly while I am at it. I feel my pussy clench at the thought of great sex and I moan. Maybe I need to get bit and get laid. I don't even care which order those happen in. My decision made, I use his shampoo and conditioner on my hair, knowing good and well that it will be frizzy without some leave-in for after the shower.

Maybe I have something in my purse? I let the conditioner soak into my hair while I soap up the rest of me. The temptation to stay and rub myself to contentment is strong, but I hold off for the bigger payoff of sex with a person I don't despise. Someone here is bound to be willing and able. Hell, I enjoy being bit, so if that is a kink they have, we could kill two birds with one stone.

I finish rinsing myself and my hair. Fuck. Where are the towels? Does he use towels or just drip dry? Ah, I see one. It is folded on a shelf under the sink. Perfect. I pad over there and grab the towel. I pat myself dry with a towel that actually absorbs water and then wrap it around myself. There have been no noises out there, but who knows? It occurs to me as I leave the bathroom for my clothes that I am thinking I need to hide my body from a guy I would very much like to have sex with. I was definitely with Fabio for entirely too long. I kept my body hidden from him as a matter of course, ever since he stopped wanting me. It was around that time that he became so mean. I still don't know why. Why he just stopped wanting me, that is. I gained a little weight and I am definitely not a teenager anymore. Even so, overnight, he just didn't want me anymore.

I realize I am standing here in this fabulous house dwelling on the bullshit of a man so out of touch with himself that he couldn't even confront his own demons before they came calling. I drop the towel and am bent over to collect my clothing when I hear the door open. Straightening and looking back, I see it's Mikael. He sees me as a grin spreads across my face. He stops in the entryway. I watch his pupils grow till I can only see a thin ring of blue around them. My gaze travels over his broad shoulders, down to his tapered waist and lands on the bulge growing in the front of his pants. I lick my lips. This could happen so much quicker than I thought possible.

"Are you just going to hang out in the entry or would you like to... come... inside?" I ask and before inside clears my lips, the door is shut, and he is standing before me, only a breath separating his cold body from my hot one. Tipping my face up to him, "Go ahead, touch me," I whisper, "I don't mind if you bite." I lean up on my toes, placing my hands on those amazing pecs for balance; I kiss the line of his jaw until his hand weaves its way into my hair and pulls me back, but keeps me on my toes. My pussy is suddenly dripping wet and his eyes drift closed as he inhales my scent. He floats closer, his other arm going around my waist to lift and crush me against his body. I can feel the hard length of his cock and I moan with the idea of getting that in my throbbing pussy.

Just as his lips near my neck he freezes, my heart sinks. He carefully sets me down and steps back, saying, "We can't do this."

"Why the hell not? Wait, do you have a girlfriend or something? Because my husband is pretty dead. He might not like it, but I don't have a single fuck to give about his opinion anymore."

"It's..." he sighs, "It's just complicated in ways you wouldn't understand. Why are you naked?"

He turns away from me to face the wall. Well, at least he wants me, even if his fucking morals are going to get in the way of my fun. "I am naked because I just showered. In your bathroom. All that gloriously hot water running over my soapy body."

He groans, "You aren't getting dressed now, though? What is stopping you now?"

I grin. This is kind of great. "My clothes are dirty. You wouldn't want me to put dirty clothing on fresh pussy now, would you?" I ask as I fold my arms under my breasts to push them up and out.

He shakes his head and disappears through the door to the left of the bathroom. Coming back out, I watch him struggle to keep his eyes on the floor while he brings me a pair of joggers and a plain white tee. Accepting the clothes from him, I turn and lay the shirt on the bed while I lean down extra to better display my ass as I get the joggers on my feet. I pull them up so slowly as I straighten and I feel his coolness behind me. Pushing my hair to one side, I tip my head to expose my neck to him. He leans in and I feel his mouth open as my eyes drift closed. Then he rips himself away to the other side of the room. Breathing heavily and pressing himself against the wall, he tells me, "You don't know what you are getting into. We can't do this. You're a human."

Shoving my arms into the shirt, I pause before pulling it over my head to retort, "You could fix that and my long dry streak all in one fell thrust. You might even enjoy it. It certainly looks like I am not the only one in need of a good lay."

He growls at me, "I need to introduce you to the rest of the vampires here. Make sure they know you are under my protection." He moves to the door so fast I barely see a blur before he is holding it open, saying, "Let's go."

I saunter over to him, pop up and kiss his chin before stepping back to say, "I know you want me. You should definitely take a bite. I am damn tasty. Oh," I move my hair and point at the spot where neck and shoulder meet, "I love being bitten right here. For future reference."

His brows drop as his scowl deepens, "Out, you heathen. We are not having sex. It would complicate things."

A man walking down the hall stops, saying, "Did you just tell her you wouldn't have sex with her? Why? Darlin," he walks over to me, "if you decide it doesn't have to be him, I beg of you, come see me. I can guarantee I will not lose my mind and say no."

Mikael growls, "Back off, Sebastian, she's mine." He runs a hand over his eyes. "Sebastian, this is Jasmine. Jasmine, this is Sebastian. Jasmine is a human. She will stay here till I can figure out what to do about the gang after her. She is off limits, understand?"

I look at him with my jaw hanging and my brows scrunched, I ask, "Are you daft? You don't get to say who can or can't have sex with me. That is my choice. And what does my being human have to do with it?"

He leans down to get in my face and says, "We eat humans."

"Oh no, don't eat me. Every woman's nightmare right there. We just hate being eaten." I raise an eyebrow at him as Sebastian laughs loud and long.

"Mikael, I think you have just met the one person on the planet, completely unfazed by you." He turns to me, saying, "Jasmine, such a pleasure meeting you. Please let me know if there are," his eyes flick down my body before coming back up to meet mine, "any ways in which I could serve a treat such as yourself." He bows and continues on his way, leaving me there to grin after him while Mikael glares at me.

Four

JASMINE

HIS POSSESSIVENESS IS annoying and only makes me want to see exactly what Sebastian could do for me. If only to spite Mikael and show him I am not a thing to be owned. Railed, yes. Owned, no. We follow Sebastian down the stairs, but where he leaves the house, we head for a room to the right of the stairs. Opening a door, he leads me into a library and I am in love. There are books everywhere. I could stay here for a year or three and read them all. I step further in, staring up at the second floor of books, stopping only when I hear a woman's voice.

"You brought home a woman?" I look for the speaker and I find two women staring at me in amazement. One has flaming red hair in a pixie cut with cat-like golden eyes and tawny skin while the other has oak-brown skin, deep brown eyes you could lose your soul in, and shoulder length dark brown hair. They are both hot as sin and remind me of how much I love women. I tune in as I realize Mikael is introducing me.

"Yes, I brought her home. There is a gang that wants to kill her. She is going to stay with us for a while. Jasmine, the one with the normal hair, is Scarlett. The lit candle is Chloe."

"It's very nice to meet you," I say as I stride over to them to shake hands.

They watch in amazement and as they shake hands with me, Scarlett says, "She isn't afraid of us at all?"

"Do not get her started. She has already asked me to turn her. Twice. I. Do. Not. Need the headache."

I pipe in right then, "I would not mind at all if Chloe or Scarlett wanted to bite me."

Scarlett looks me up and down, then says to Mikael with a smile, "Bold, isn't she? I like it. Let's see how insane you make him, then we can talk about biting. In the meantime, what are you going to feed her? We have alcohol and blood in this house. You know that will not keep a human alive, right?"

"Shit. Yes. I do. But I haven't had time to get anything. I'll order in for her tonight." I watch all this conversation about me with some amusement, and Chloe winks at me when she notices.

Chloe tells me, "He is going to forget to get you food. Don't let him and make sure he knows you need more than one meal a night. Vampires forget being human, especially when they are as ancient as he is."

Mikael's jaw drops, and he says, "Are you calling me old?"

Scarlett raises an expertly sculpted brow at him, saying,

"If the shoe fits, I guess you better lace that bitch up and own it."

I am struggling at this point not to laugh at him. He shakes his head, "Ok. I brought her in to introduce you to her so you wouldn't eat her—"

"I would be ok with being eaten. Especially if I get to return the favor."

Chloe and Scarlett bust out laughing while Mikael just puts his hands to his head and rubs his temples before he says, "Come on. I need to introduce you to the guys. Fuck me, what have I gotten myself into?"

I laugh as he heads for the door, saying to the women, "It was really nice meeting you both. I hope to spend some quality time with you soon."

Chloe calls out as I turn to leave, "Quality time with whom?"

I pause and look over my shoulder, saying, "Either. Or both. I'm game."

I find Mikael out in the hall and as he leads me toward the back of the house he asks, "Is there anyone you won't flirt with?"

"Probably, but I haven't found them yet. Although, I would like to point out that I didn't flirt with any of the guys that were surrounding my car this morning. So you don't have coffee here either, do you?"

He pulls out his phone, grumbling, "No. I don't drink it. I'll get some stuff ordered from a delivery service. Are you particular about what coffee you drink?"

"It has to be caffeinated. I will murder you over decaf. I need cream and sugar to go with it. And food. I am hungry. I need food soon."

He taps away at his phone screen as we enter the kitchen. This kitchen is gourmet, like wow. I would love to cook in here. Holy shit. I don't even care if the only thing currently in the fridge is blood. I can see that blood is all that is in there because he has a fridge with glass doors. The stove is huge and I could make all the things. I finally notice three guys standing around an island as my gaze travels over the expanse of the kitchen. Two brunettes and a blond. They wave. Mikael is still engrossed in the order he is making on his phone.

I walk over and stick my hand out to shake at the blond one, saying, "Hi, I'm Jasmine. You are?"

The blond one replies, "I'm Asher. These two are Eason and Quinn. What's Mikael so distracted by?"

"He's ordering me food. Sad, sad fact of the human condition. We have to be fed regularly. And we need caffeine. So he is getting me supplies for..." I turn to look back at Mikael, "How long are you planning for me to stay here?"

"What? Oh, um, indefinitely. You have an entire gang looking for you. You were a witness to them killing many people."

"Well, they were just eating, and I said I wouldn't tell. It's not like I cared about any of them."

"Not even your husband?" He asks as he goes back to his phone.

I decide not to answer him since he is obviously not interested, but the other three are looking at me when I turn back to them, shrugging as I say, "What? He was mean as hell, rarely had sex with me and when he did, it was not what anyone would call worth the wait. So no, I didn't care anymore. I was saving up to leave him. Now that he is dead, it actually makes my life easier. No watching over my shoulder for him coming to collect me."

The three of them look pretty fucking grim now, and one of the brunettes, Eason I think, says, "You should stay till you are on your feet. Do you have family?"

"No. My parents died a long time ago and the one aunt I had wanted to sell my body for drug money. So, with my husband dead, it's just little ol' me here."

"Hmm," Asher rubs his jaw, "you would make a fine candidate for turning. Why aren't you a vampire yet? You got here this morning, right?"

"I did, and slept my way through the day." Flipping my hair back over my shoulder, I say, "If you are offering to turn me, my preferred place for biting is here." I say, pointing to the juncture of shoulder and neck.

All of their eyes get a shade darker as they look at my exposed neck. I have never felt so wanted as I do right now. It doesn't even matter that I would be a meal, as long as they turned me after. I feel Mikael step up behind me and the guys all avert their eyes as he says, "She is off limits. No one bites her. Understand?"

"Of course." "Yes." "Yes."

I narrow my eyes at Mikael, saying, "What the fuck? You don't want to turn me and you won't let anyone else turn me, either? Why the hell not? What reason could there possibly be for keeping me human?"

"I... you... just... You are too good a person to be one of us! I won't have the turning of an innocent on my conscience!"

I laugh then, "Oh honey, all the good Christian women

that used to live in my trailer park could tell you. Innocent, I'm not. I've been to jail for assault three times, and those are just the ones they could prove. My aunt was trying to sell me when I was still a kid and I married my husband, at least in part, to get out of there. Don't get me wrong, I loved him back then. But I would have married just about anyone to get the emancipation that marriage afforded me." I take a deep breath to calm down. Damn it, I didn't realize I would get emotional over this. I dab at the corners of my eyes, "I am not an innocent. Where's my fucking coffee?"

Mikael smirks at me, saying, "It just got here. I'll get it."

Asher waits till Mikael has been gone a few minutes, saying, "We'll help you convince him. Even if somehow we can't, we know others. We can guide you to vampires that would help. Ah, here he comes back with your coffee."

A minute later, Mikael comes into the kitchen with multiple large bags dangling from his hands. He sets them all on a counter and gestures for me to take over. I dive in, seeking the coffee maker first. Setting that aside, I dig out coffee and filters. In no time, I have the coffee maker set up and brewing coffee. That done, I pull the rest out of the bags, happy to see I will eat well for the next week. Turning to Mikael, I ask, "Where should I put the things that need to stay cold? I don't mind if they are in with your blood, but is that ok with you?"

"Yes, it's fine. Just shove the blood off to the side."

Quinn shoots Mikael a pointed look that he ignores. With a huff, Quinn goes to the fridge, opens a door and starts stacking the blood off to one side, saying, "Don't worry. Some of us haven't lost our manners. I'll make a space for you. Here, hand me the things that need to go in here."

I scoop up the meat and veggies, I'll make sure to cook the veggies since they will all be together. Then I hand them over to Quinn, who sets them all carefully into the space he just cleared out.

The coffee maker stops and I ask, "Are there any cups here?"

* * *

Sometime later I am fed, and caffeinated, following Mikael to his office so we can discuss things. I have a variety of things I want to discuss with him. Who knows what he wants to discuss? On the far side of the house, he enters a room and stands next to the door while I enter. He shuts the door behind me and walks over to the fireplace. With a button push, he has it going. I move to stand in front of it as they keep the temperature pretty low in this house.

He gestures toward a small bar, asking me, "Would you like something to drink?"

"Yes, please. So blood and alcohol is pretty much it for you all?" I ask, looking around at his space. It is pretty neutral. His space doesn't seem hyper masculine like so many men's offices. There are decorative pieces and pretty curtains. I wonder if maybe he has a girlfriend? Boyfriend? Something? The chairs are a lighter green color and, much like the ones in his bedroom, very cushy looking.

He brings me a drink, saying, "Here you go. And yes, alcohol and blood are pretty much it for us. Though the alcohol doesn't do much for us beyond being something different."

He sits in one chair while I sip my drink with my back to the flames. This is the best whiskey I have ever tasted. I take a few more sips and feel a delicious warmth spreading through my belly. Feeling plenty warm, I move to sit in the chair opposite him. I look up to find him watching me; the firelight reflecting in his eyes. Good grief, I would do him for a day old donut and cold coffee.

Clearing my throat, I start the ball rolling, asking, "So, how long do you think I will need to stay here?"

He swirls his whiskey, "I don't know. I am not in the habit of taking in humans. I haven't run into this issue before."

"Why did you agree? You started out telling me to carry on, but changed your mind. Why?"

He sips his whiskey, eyes down so I can't read whatever information could be gleaned from them. "I don't know exactly. Maybe you remind me of someone I used to know. I will do some checking to see how long he tends to hold a grudge or try to eliminate witnesses. In the meantime, you are safe here. You will have my room to sleep in and no one will bother you while you are here."

"Thanks, that is reassuring. How will I get my things? What happens when he finds out you are not actually claiming me? Wouldn't this be solved by making me one of you?"

"They burnt that trailer park to the ground. You don't have any things left there to get or I would send someone to pick it all up. He won't find out that I am not claiming you anytime soon. You will still have my protection. It might be solved that way, but I am not turning you, nor will I allow anyone else to do so."

My eyes narrow. The audacity on this man. Fine. At least I have a backup plan. "Fine. And where will you be sleeping? I still would not be averse to sharing a bed with you."

He slants a look at me, saying, "I will sleep on a couch here in the house."

"You prefer to sleep on a couch? Or do you have a special someone?"

"I don't sleep a lot to begin with, but no, I do not prefer a couch. No, I do not have a special someone. I wanted to give you privacy and space."

With a sigh, I say, "I'd rather have that dick." Finishing my drink in one swallow and standing, I say, "I am going to go to that very lonely bed. I still think you should join me there, but since you won't, do you have a blanket to throw over those sheets? I get cold all by myself."

He raises a brow at me since we both know he is cold, "There are blankets in the closet, feel free to use whichever one you like."

I set my glass down on the bar and saunter my ass out of there. I wonder if anyone else is still awake?

Five

JASMINE

I WAKE up that evening all snugged up under this really fluffy blanket I found, feeling comfy and warm. Sitting up, I realize that I don't have clothing for today, unless I raid his closet some more. Grabbing my phone and pulling up a website, I have all that money in savings and this is the kind of thing it should be for. I spend some time adding items to the cart. I am still cost conscious, even if I don't need to runaway anymore. There, got the last items added to the cart and now I can... not checkout because I don't know the address here. Fuck. As I get up to finally visit the bathroom, his clothes from yesterday are still laying on the foot of the bed. I think about putting them on but nah, I am in a room by myself. I'll dress when I leave the room.

Just as I get to the door of the bathroom I hear the bedroom door open and Mikael swearing, "Fuck, don't you ever wear clothing?"

I laugh, saying, "Yes, but I need clothing to wear. Put

the address in the boxes on the phone so I can get my order here." I step into the bathroom and leave him to it. I really had to go and ah, the sweet relief. Cleaning up and washing my hands, I am careful to hang the towel back up when I finish. He hands me the phone when I get to the bed. I look at the screen. Looks like he put the order through. Excellent. Hopefully, it was still set to fast shipping. I hit the button to shut off the display and look up to see him staring at me like he wants to eat me. Deciding to let him chase me this time, I pick up his shirt. When I straighten, I find him standing much closer. I drop the shirt and put my hands on that big chest of his, raising up on my toes to whisper in his ear, "I taste just as good as I look. Go ahead, run your hands down my body," I feel his hands settle on my waist and one goes up my back while the other runs down to cup my ass. His cock is pressing into my stomach through his pants and I press my body against it, making him groan. The hand on my back moves to cup a breast before pinching my nipple lightly. I gasp and moan softly in his ear, "Yesss."

I press soft kisses on his collarbone as his hands continue to explore my body. Just as things are getting exciting, some jackass knocks on the door and he freezes. He steps back from me, grasping my arms when I wobble because I was leaning on him. His face is flushed and his fangs out, his eyes are more pupil than anything as he calls out, "Yes, who is it?"

"It's Eason. Some information came to me and I wanted to share. Is this not a good time?"

Mikael's eyes flit down my body and back up to meet mine. He says, "I'll be right out. Meet me in the kitchen."

I smirk, "Suddenly hungry? You could take care of that here, you know."

He leans in and takes a deep breath with his nose buried in my neck. I lean my head away to give him better access, but he withdraws. "I'll see you downstairs. Help yourself to my closet until your clothes arrive."

"Ugh. Fine. Do you have a washer set?"

"Yes, it is down the hall, the door is marked laundry."

"Good. I'll wash my clothes and the ones of yours I wore last night. Hard to keep my pants dry with you all around."

His eyes widen and he smiles, chuckling as he walks to the door and leaves the room. Blast it all, Eason, I was getting there. I sigh and head for his closet. Fuck, it's big. He has a lot of nice button up shirts. I decide to try one of those tied at the bottom and a stretchy pair of running pants. Yes, these fit me nicely since they are supposed to be form fitted, and the shirt works tied up with not all the buttons done up. I straighten up the bed and gather my laundry, heading down the hall to find this washing set.

Six

JASMINE

LATER THAT NIGHT, Chloe and Scarlett have found
me in the library, and they have questions. I tell them the
story of how I found Mikael by accident, running from tall,
dark, and deadly. They are fascinated by Mikael's response
to me because he has never brought a woman home. They
chose to live here and requested to be part of his clan, since
it seemed the safest.

Chloe says, "We actually kind of thought he might just
not be interested in women at all after the first fifty or so
years."

I grin, "Nope. I can assure you, he is very much interested in women. I almost had him today, but Eason
knocked on the door and brought him to his senses."

Scarlett laughs, saying, "You're trying to bed him? Even
after his pronouncements?"

My smile gets wider. I tell them, "Yes, yes I am. The

hope is that he will have sex with me, which I really need and after or during, he will turn me. I want to be a vampire and I think it will solve a lot of problems for me."

Chloe nods, saying, "It really does in so many ways. I mean, there are still problems with being a vampire, but they don't really compare with the problems of being a human woman."

"Exactly. So, I plan to convince him one way or another. I am focusing on him because he forbade all of you. Is there anything I should know about the process? About what happens after I am turned?"

Scarlett shrugs at Chloe and says, "There are things you need to know and since you plan to convince him to turn you in the heat of the moment, you should know these things beforehand." Chloe nods and Scarlett continues, "The process, that's pretty cut and dried. You get drained, then you get fed the vampire blood. It's really straightforward. After that, most of us just try to sleep while our bodies change. It isn't the most pleasant thing ever, but it isn't the worst thing ever either."

Chloe laughs, saying, "A few days later, when the memories come in is when it really gets interesting. Most people run into certain others again and again as they move through different incarnations. We very often have not finished something with them. Normal stuff. But when the memories from those lives come in, they feel very now. All the emotions from those memories are overwhelming. Like finding out the woman that is your mother this time was the judge at your hanging trial a couple of lifetimes ago. Or your shitty neighbor was your beloved at some point. That has occasionally caused some problems. We can let most of what we remember go. It is very rare that we need to act on the memories that emerge."

"Rare? Meaning some memories need to be taken care of? Can I get an example?"

Scarlett chuckles softly, "Well, for instance, if you run into the man that owned you in another life and he was just as repulsive a person in this one, you might be justified in checking to see if the evil was in his blood or if it was just his soul. Of course, you would have to drink every drop to be sure." She smiles, "Turns out it was definitely the soul."

I laugh with Chloe and it occurs to me I should be more afraid of the people I am so casually conversing with, but I can't find any fear of these people. These people, the ones the rest of the world refer to as monsters, have been kinder to me than any of the fine, upstanding citizens I have ever been associated with, starting with my aunt. She went to church three times a week and was considered a godly woman. Some of those same people that she attended church with were the ones trying to buy me or spend time with me when I was still a kid. My husband was thought to be a good guy by everyone that knew him, even the ones that saw him hit me. One of them told me I should try to be more agreeable.

But these monsters, as people would have them labeled, they kill on a regular basis to survive. The same as everyone else does. I am going to need to think about this more, because I don't mind becoming a monster. Everyone thinks I am a degenerate already, it looks like monster might be a step up.

Chloe says, "We have a running theory that we get all the memories back because we are out of the loop as vampires. The soul journey has taken a sharp left turn and now must go about things differently."

"I like that idea. So what is Mikael's big reason for not turning me? If you know, that is."

Chloe laughs, "Well, what had happened was, he thinks he is damned for becoming a vampire. That we all are really. He feels people cannot possibly understand what they are getting into and therefore must not even be given the decision to make."

"Wait, what? He just decided that he knows best for everyone? Really?"

Scarlett nods, saying, "He really did. He has never let go of the audacity he was born into, so it has just gotten worse with time. He means well but could honestly stand to learn. A lot."

"Wow, he is so much less hot knowing about all that audacity in him. Oh well, it should be fun for a time to 'help' him learn how to act right."

Chloe and Scarlett laugh long and loud at that, Chloe saying, "Oh girl, this is going to be the best telenovela I have seen in a long time. Get him. And if he doesn't turn you soon, we will. We stay here for convenience. Not because we have to and we don't mind leaving with a new sister of the blood."

"You two are the best. I feel like I need to push him into changing me, but if we have sex and somehow he still avoids turning me, I will be coming to find you. For now, I need food. The human condition requires multiple feedings daily. I will see you both soon. Thanks for helping me get informed. You are both appreciated so much."

They wave me off, looking uncomfortable with the thanks so I just get myself out of there because I don't want to make them uncomfortable.

Seven

JASMINE

IN THE KITCHEN, I am blasting some music on my phone while I make food. It is strange cooking for just myself, but I can't say I don't like it. Today I am having sauteed greens with a pork chop on the side and some acorn squash. I need to order some more food now that I have the address. Food going, I turn to my phone and lower the volume since it will be so close. I raise my eyes to the ceiling. It's a really nice ceiling, and try to think of what stores would be good to order from. After I finally decide on a store and drag my eyes from the ceiling to find Sebastian in front of me. I jump, "Fucking shit! Don't sneak up on people like that! I am still human, I coulda had a heart attack!"

Sebastian laughs, "I was trying to see what you were looking at up there. What are you doing? You need to tend your food before it burns."

"Dammit!" I set my phone on the counter to go move

stuff around in the pan. "I was thinking. That ceiling is really great, and I was using it for inspiration."

He looks up at the ceiling. "Its just a ceiling."

I look over at him, saying, "No, it is not. To me, that is a great ceiling. All smooth and designs and scrollwork around the edges. Way above stained ceiling tiles and tin that has been silver-queened so much the thin walls of the trailer are barely holding up the weight of it. But the water just keeps finding a way in."

He eyes me and the ceiling in turns, saying, "I suppose it differs from what you describe. I haven't been in a trailer at all. I think I have lived a much different life than you."

I set my greens on a plate, saying, "How surprising. How old are you? Are you thousands of years old? Hundreds?"

"A few hundred." He leans against the counter as I set my pork chop on the plate, saying, "Definitely before the time of trailers."

I open the oven and use a towel to pull out the acorn squash, "As I suspected. Much too old to remember being poor, if you ever were."

"Well, you've got me there. I was never what one would call poor. I was the son of a nobleman when I was turned. An absolute cad, but I had a charming, rakish air about me, so people let it slide. Women adored me, at first." He chuckled, "And then there was a new woman and they would hate me for a time. It didn't matter to me. I was young and having fun. Then one night on my drunken way home, I was stopped by a gorgeous woman who said she needed my assistance. I followed her right up to her quarters and there my fate was sealed."

I laugh while I butter the squash and then carry plate and utensils to the island. I sit on a stool and start cutting my chop. "So some fabulous lady of the night walked up to you and said, I need your assistance and you just followed along like a good pup, never even the slightest clue, no thought that this might be a trap?"

Sebastian shakes his head ruefully, "Sadly, no. I was, regrettably, as dumb as I was young. But here I am now. I think it all worked out."

"Looks like. What was being turned like for you? Why did she turn you? Did she give you any guidance after?"

His eyes widen at my questions. He asks, "So you really mean to be turned?"

"I asked you first, but yes. I am working on a plan to get Mikael to turn me, unless," I tip my head to the side and move the hair from my neck, "you would like to take care of that now?"

His eyes glitter and I watch his fangs extend, he says, "Put that away. Eat your food. You know Mikael has forbidden all of us to bite you."

I shrug, "I mean, we could have sex and you could do it in the heat of the moment. I would be happy to swear it was an accident." His eyes still glitter and the pupils are large. The fangs have gone nowhere. Fuck it, I'm shooting my shot. I get up and walk over to stand in front of him, asking, "Can I put my hands on you?"

He sucks in air even as he nods. I place my splayed hands on his chest and rise on my toes, my mouth a hairsbreadth from his, I whisper, "Can I kiss you?" He answers with his arms crushing my body to his as his lips meet mine in a kiss that could set fire to a thousand ships. His cock is digging into my belly as he lifts me off my feet. My nails dig into his chest as his other hand roams my back to settle on my ass.

He breaks the kiss, gasping for air and growling as he sets me down and away from him, his hands on my arms, he says, "I am not strong enough for this." For long moments, the only sound is our heavy breathing.

"You could. You could definitely do this. I really want you to do this. And I will absolutely be grateful if you turn me before, during, or after. Please do this. Don't leave me hanging..."

He looks me in the eye. The hunger I see there sends a rush of heat to my core. He says, "I want to, oh god do I want to. Mikael has all but claimed you. I can't interfere with that. He doesn't own you, I know, I know. But I do owe him. And oh, is the debt being paid right now. Please understand that my walking away from you right now is nothing," the growl that comes out as he says nothing gives me the most delicious shivers, "about me not wanting to finish this. I assure you, I very much want you."

He releases my arms and leaves the kitchen so fast I don't even see him go. And I am left with a throbbing pussy and cold food. I finish the food, because I need to eat. While I force that down my throat, I sit there getting more angry in time with the throbbing of my aching pussy. I have never been turned down so many times in all my life. What the fuck is up with this place?

After my food is finished, I clean up and head upstairs. It's almost morning and I need to get some sleep since there appears to be no chance I am getting any dick or vagina tonight. Stomping my way up the stairs I run into Chloe, she says something to me and I just grunt as I walk on by. Suddenly I am slammed against the wall and she is whispering in my ear, "They left you hanging, not me. But I'll help you out," I feel her hand slipping in the waistband of Mikael's pants and slipping down to press my clit, "because I can't stand to see a girl so miserable." With that, she slips two fingers into my soaked pussy, pressing the base of her thumb against my clit as she fucks me with her fingers. I moan, "Oh yes, yes, yes!" She speeds up her ministrations and I cum on her talented fingers within a couple minutes, thankfully she keeps me pressed against the wall with her arm across my chest because my legs forget how to support me. I recover the ability to stand and make coherent sounds, and she extracts her hand from my pants, licking her fingers and grinning at me.

"Would, uh, would you like to come to my room and allow me to reciprocate?"

She grins, saying, "Ordinarily, I would say yes, but I just had sex with Eason. I was on my way to the shower. I'll take a raincheck for a later date though."

"Well, then thank you. I feel a lot less angry suddenly and I am going to bed. You have a wonderful day and feel free to cash in that raincheck whenever you like."

She grins a little wider and continues on her way as I make my way to my, well, Mikael's room. I walk in and find my clothing order sitting on the bed. Wonderful. I move it off to one side and after visiting the bathroom; I press the button to turn off the lamp and fall into bed, snuggling in as sleep comes easily for once.

. . .

Mikael

I have avoided Jasmine all night by hiding in my office. I want her so badly I can taste her blood on my tongue already. But she isn't my wife, I would feel it if she were. I have every other time I got anywhere near her. My wife has not been back in many years and I am beginning to wonder if maybe she isn't coming back this time. Maybe she moved on since I couldn't bring myself to take her from any of her happy homes. I miss her. I should have let her see me, let her know me, and make the choice.

I may never see her again and I will have no one to blame but myself. Why didn't I ever just introduce myself to her? Any one of the times that she was reborn. Ah love, why aren't you back yet?

I hear Jasmine stomping up the stairs, ridiculous behavior considering she hasn't seen me since this morning. She is still human and they are so flighty, they barely have time to know their own minds before they are dead and gone. Silly mortal. Still, she draws me like no other. I should be ashamed of my weakness for her. I know the others are surprised that I brought her home at all and more surprised that I marked her off limits to everyone.

I don't know if I will be able to hold them to any sort of consequences if they ignore my edicts. She is not interested in belonging to me alone, not that I would want her to be mine alone. The thought is laughable. She has no idea of the world, young as she... How old is she?

It matters not. She is off to sleep for the day and I am tired too. I worked through the hunger for her body by throwing myself into the accounts and they are all in order now. But I neglected to go out and feed. I am stuck with blood from a bag because if I go out now, one of that little gang leader's watchers might spot me. They watch the house all day and the little gangbangers come out to watch the place at night. Jasmine will be safe as long as she stays inside. He will assume her dead after so long and then she should be able to go on with her life.

I feel a sharp pain in my chest at the thought of her leaving. How is that even possible? She is nothing to me. Just some tempting curves wrapped in scents that make me hard to think of them. I launch myself out of my office chair, landing across the room in front of the door. Opening it, I step through and close it behind. The kitchen is across the house and toward the rear. I smell the scent of Jasmine on the air as I pass the stairs. Odd, but maybe she got sweaty, expending all the energy to stomp up those stairs.

I enter the kitchen, and I smell her again. It smells like sex, but the scents aren't mingled enough for the act to have been consummated, Sebastian. I have to talk to her about not going after the other vampires here, after I forbade them from having her. I can't even blame Sebastian for having trouble saying no to her. She is... persuasive. Grabbing a bag of blood, I bite into it and head for the sitting room I have been sleeping in to avoid her charms. The couch there is not the most comfortable, but it will suffice till she can go on her way.

I toss the now empty bag in the small wastebasket in the corner and lay down on the couch. It was a long night and tomorrow night isn't likely to be better.

* * *

I wake to the feeling of someone in the room. My eyes seek this intruder and it is her, my wife. My Isryana, wearing the form she wore when we were married. I stand, "My love, my love. Where have you been all this time? I have been searching everywhere for you."

Her face twists in a mask of anger as she says, "Looking for me? Why? So you can watch me from the shadows again? Leave me to whatever life I am half living while my soul searched for the one it could feel just out of reach?"

My jaw drops as I say, "You knew?"

"Every time!" She screams at me, "I could feel you watching me! I knew my other half was out there somewhere, watching me and never revealing themselves. All I could think for so long was that I must not measure up. Maybe that body wasn't good enough. Maybe I wasn't smart enough this time. But no, it was never about me. You don't know how to love! I should never have believed you when you said you would come for me!"

I fall to my knees as she screams at me. My head in my hands, "I'm sorry, I'm so sorry. I should have come to you. I should have trusted you to make your own decisions."

"Oh, you think? I'm done with you Mikael. I renounce your claim on me. If you find me in this life," she laughs, "who am I kidding? I could be right under your nose and you would never know it. You are so enamored of your own brilliance. Goodbye Mikael. May you find yourself without your overweening sense of your own brilliance."

She fades away and I wake up as I fall off the couch reaching for her, shouting, "Noooo!" I look around and realize it is barely mid-day. I lay back to sleep as best I can for the rest of the day.

Eight

JASMINE

WAKING UP TONIGHT, I linger in bed, just wishing I had someone to visit me in it. I still feel weird about jumping into a new life right after Fabio died, but I was already gone from that relationship, anyway. I'm not dwelling on a guy that was bad for me, even if his death was really convenient and could even be considered good for me. A whole wave of guilt breaks over me. Annoyed with myself, I kick off the covers, getting out of the bed to go visit the bathroom. Coming out of the bathroom, I look at the box of clothes and the bed. Do I want to try on really cute clothes I got as cheaply as possible or go continue my pity party in the bed for a little while longer?

Bed. Definitely a pity party in the bed. I crawl in the bed and just as I pull the covers over me, the bedroom door flies open to let a furious Mikael in the room. I sit up, holding the blanket to my chest as he closes the door behind him.

He turns to face me and, through clenched teeth, asks, "What in the hell are you doing having sex in the hallway?" He inhales, "And why in the fuck do you smell like two! Two! Different. Vampires."

"I thought I would see how many vampires I had to fuck before I found the one that would turn me." Oh, that made him mad, ha. Good.

He stalks closer as he says, "Maybe I should teach you a lesson about sleeping with vampires and why you shouldn't."

Teach me? Oh, motherfucker. I stand up out of the bed and meet him nose to, well, I'm looking up as I tell him, "You don't get to say who I sleep with. Not ever. I am an entire person to myself. You don't get to control my sexuality, even if we were having sex. Do you have more shitty caveman ideas floating around in there that we need to disabuse you of? Something I can clear up for you?"

"I do have control of you. This is my house. My bed. My food. And my protection. While you need those, you will do as I say!"

I laugh in his face, "Sure Dad, can I use the car Friday if I'm really good?" I roll my eyes and walk around him, saying, "You have got to be kidding me. That was really the best you could come up with? The crappy dad line? Fuuuu-uckk yooooou." I snatch the box open and start pulling out clothing.

"What are you doing?"

"Not that it is any of your business, but I am going to get dressed and then I am going to leave here for anywhere else. I don't have to stay here with you. I chose to because I felt like it would be a good thing. But noooo, you had to go fucking that up."

He looks stricken, but I choose to ignore it as I try to find the panties I bought. He comes over and grabs my arm, forcing me to turn toward him. I glare up at him, snarling, "That is my arm. Release it or I will scream till your sensitive ears bleed."

His eyes widen and he says, "I don't want you to leave. That was not my intention. I, I apologize for what I said. The smell of your climax in the hallway and I was jealous. I want you, I have my own reasons why I can't have you—"

"Oh sir, you can't have me. I am not an object. You could have taken part in having sex with me. Whatever sex means to you, I think we are in two different places with that. I do not see sex as some sort of gateway drug to a relationship. I don't want a relationship right now. Not with you or anyone else. I do very much want to have sex and I will not be saving that for a marriage that is not likely to ever happen because I don't want it to happen."

"Don't you even want to hear the rest?"

"Does it end with you telling me what you are going to do to learn how to be better? Are we going to have sex before I go? What is it you want me to hear?"

He belatedly releases my arm and looks down, seeming to realize I am standing naked in front of him. He steps back quickly, "I didn't, uh, I didn't realize you hadn't dressed yet today. Maybe I should..."

"Oh no," I say as I close the space between us, "you busted in here wanting to tell me off about my sex life. Let me just tell you all about it so you can get it right when you tell the tale someday. You left me hanging last evening for your reasons, reasons that you don't want to share. Fine. I spent the day talking with the other people here. People that weren't avoiding me." He looks surprised I knew, but I continue, "Yes, I was aware you were avoiding me. I chose not to seek you out. I cornered Sebastian in the kitchen and nearly had him, but he feels like he owes you, so he walked away." He looks a little turned on hearing this. He obviously he needs more details. "I walked up to him and put my hands on his chest like this," I place my splayed hands on his chest, "then I put my lips close to his and asked if I could kiss him." I take a step back, letting my hands fall from his chest and come to rest on my hips. "After he left me hanging too, I stomped upstairs and was rude to Chloe. She could tell I needed an orgasm. So she put me against the wall with one arm while she slipped her other hand into my pants and fingered me till I came. All. Over. Her. Hand."

I look up just in time to see him lose control. He grabs me and crushes my body to his as he kisses me with a fierceness that has me melting in all the right spots.

Nine

JASMINE

HIS HANDS ARE ROAMING every inch of my body, and I am reveling in it. He settles both hands on my ass and lifts me up so he can kiss his way down to my breasts. I hear a muffled, "Oh gods, you smell so fucking good. You taste like I could eat you up." Followed by some incoherent growls, or maybe I am the incoherent one as he sucks hard on my nipple and then lets his teeth scrape it lightly as he releases it. My moans fill the room as he moves to the other breast. I feel movement and then I am on my back on the bed and his face is between my thighs, looking down at my pussy like a starving man at the buffet.

I watch as he snatches his shirt open and yanks it off. He leans down and slips his tongue between my pussy lips and into me as far as he can, then he pulls back and licks all the way up, stopping with his tongue pressed flat against my aching clit. He flicks his tongue while keeping it pressed against my clit and I almost cum on his face. Mikael circles my clit with his tongue while he slips three fingers into me. He hooks his fingers and starts fucking me with them as his devil mouth sucks hard on my clit and the orgasm slams into me, leaving me in a shaking, dripping mess.

He releases the suction when my body shakes like a washing machine. When the shaking subsides, he slips his fingers from me and stands. I open my eyes and tell him, "You better not be leaving, I swear—"

He chuckles and releases the catch on his pants, opening them and dropping them to the floor. His cock is pretty magnificent. I have high hopes for this one. He crawls over me, every inch the predator. I let my legs drop open and rock my pelvis to make the angle better as he guides himself into me. The feel of that glorious stretch of being slowly filled as he enters me so slowly, I could die from the pleasure of it. I watch as it enters me. It is mesmerizing. I hear his breath catch and I look up at him.

He is holding his breath, eyes scrunched closed, and biting his lip. Oh, so it's like that? I give my hips a quick little twist, and he moans. I do it again and he buries his cock in me, making me gasp even as he growls. Planting my feet and rocking my pelvis slowly, I watch his eyes roll back in his head. When I have withdrawn him as far as I can from me, I slam back up on him and he roars, clutching my body tightly. He fucks me hard and fast as he buries his fangs in my neck. The bite sends me over the edge and I cum again, sending him to new heights as he growls while he drinks from me and fucks me. Oh fuck me, if this is how I die, I must have been a really good girl in this life.

I feel myself getting weaker as he drinks deeply from

me. All I can hope for as my vision dims is that he turns me before I can't be turned.

I can hear him off in the distance. Why is he so far away, I wonder? I feel so nice, I could float here. I feel so light. A liquid hits the back of my throat and I choke a little, coughing. Then I am ravenous for the liquid. It is all fire and life, and I need more now. Wish granted, the flow of liquid finds me again and I drink greedily. I feel so strong, so fed. Grabbing the thing, an arm? I press it into my mouth as I drink deeply.

Finally, I am sated. I smile and release the flow of life. I hear Mikael saying, "Are you okay? Did it work?" He grabs my arms and shakes me a little.

I open my eyes and smile at him, saying, "Did what work? The orgasm? Because yes. The liquid life you poured down my throat? That seems to have done the trick too. I feel much more alive now than I did a few minutes ago. Why?"

"Oh thank the gods, I thought I was too late. I think I almost was. I wasn't sure if you would come back. But I didn't realize I was biting you until it was nearly too late."

I smile again, "That's ok. You just relax. I'm going to nap now. The girls told me naps are best after you get turned."

"Good, good. Get some sleep. Just, ah hell, I'm so sorry. I never meant to turn you."

"Shut up. You are ruining a perfectly good post orgasmic glow." I close my eyes and slip off to sleep.

Ten

JASMINE

I WAKE TO MIKAEL HOVERING, which is odd since his usual MO is to avoid me. "Can I help you?"

"How do you feel?"

"Like you're hovering and I just woke up. Give me some space, jeez."

He scoots back almost a whole inch on the bed. "I wasn't sure. Couldn't be sure you would wake up. I couldn't be certain that I got you in time."

Shit. He was concerned for me. I'm an asshole. I sit up, marveling at how easy this is as a vampire. "You got me in time. I am fine. You did good," I say as I reach over and give him a hug. He wraps his arms around me and drags me into his lap. Hmm, this is nice. I could cuddle up here and relax for a while. But that might give him the wrong idea. I still don't want a relationship with him. Even if he rails me right.

I start to squirm after a few moments, saying, "Listen, I need to get dressed. And I am feeling a little peckish."

"Can you ever forgive me?"

I lean back to look at him, asking, "What? Forgive you for what?"

"For turning you."

My eyes roll before I can stop them. I tell him, "Oh for fuck's sake. How are you still on about this? I wanted to be a vampire. You did exactly what I hoped you would do." I crawl out of his lap and go back to my box, now on the floor. Picking it up, I go back to searching for the panties and the bra.

"I need to tell you the reason why I stopped turning anyone." He looks very serious as I put on my panties.

I decide laughter is probably not the best reaction, so I tell him, "Go ahead. It probably isn't as terrible as you think it is."

"We'll see if you still feel that way after. I was turned," I tip my head because he feels like he lied just there, but what could be a lie about being turned? I pay more attention as he continues, "as a way to take my estates from me. A wizard had my wife murdered and had me turned so that I could find her again. I became this, and he became the new lord of my manor. I was angry for a long time and I vowed I would get my revenge on him. It took many years of waiting, watching, and building my own army, but I attacked and took the castle. Then I hunted him down and drank my fill of his blood. My fill was when he died."

I nod as I pull the crop top over my head, saying, "Can't say I blame you. I assume you loved the wife. It sounds like you did right by her in death, if not in life."

He nods, "Yes, I did. But taking the wizard's life had an effect."

"Wait, is that why you can be in the sun?"

"Yes, that is one of the things that came from it. I also can do some magic, probably more if I trained at it."

"That is pretty cool, in my opinion." I tell him as I shimmy into the pleather skirt I ordered. Already knowing what kind of job I will be going after and this is exactly the right outfit to get me hired. I'll need to visit a drugstore for some makeup. "Can you change my hair color?"

He looks up at me, asking, "What?"

"The magic, is it useful? Can you change my hair color with it?"

"Yes, probably? But that isn't the point. The point of this deep confession," he glares at me, brows down and his little mouth pouty, "is that the magic is against the laws of nature, with it I am doubly cursed and I may have passed this curse on to you."

He is really serious about this. Oh boy. Don't laugh Jasmine. Giggle later. "I forgive you, and I absolve you of all responsibility for this, as it was something I was pushing to have happen. It's all my fault, really. You should probably be mad at me."

He shakes his head, saying, "I can't be mad at you. You thought I was just a vampire, you couldn't have guessed at the rest of it. Besides, it was me that forbade anyone else from turning you because I was jealous. I should take you for your first feeding. Now that you are turned, it is my duty to make sure that you are capable and ready for all that this life throws at you. And if you reveal the extra things you inherited from me, you will have to die."

I nod as I finish sliding on some heeled boots. I save the spike-heeled shoes for when I go try out. For now, I need better balance and the thicker heels of these boots will provide that while helping me adjust to the heeled life. "Sounds good. Let's go get me some take out." I turn and grin at him, but he doesn't get it at all. He thinks I'm serious. What a giant stick he must have up his ass. Or maybe I am just too much right now and super inappropriate? "It was a joke, because I'll be taking them out?"

"Oh, I thought, well, never mind what I thought. Let's go."

He leads the way. We walk quickly toward the lower downtown area. It is the place where a lot more goes on than people that live in the fancy apartments two blocks away like to think about, so likely the best place to find the kind of person I am likely to be ok with un-aliving.

Mikael says, "Her, she would be good. Not too strong and she is alone."

I see a woman plying the trade on an unusual corner. There are no others around her, and she looks scared. Looking at him, I say, "Nah. I'm not preying on someone already down on their luck. Nobody working a desolate corner is ok, she doesn't even have any witnesses if some whacked out asshole beats her to death or takes her for that ride she never comes back from. I will not prey on her. And if you do, we are gonna fight."

He raises an eyebrow, saying, "Sounds like the monster doesn't want to be the bad guy."

I walk off, telling him, "I don't mind the label monster. All the monsters I have ever met were much better people than the fine upstanding ones I saw in church and when they came to my aunt's house to try to buy time with me. I think maybe our societal understanding of what makes a monster is flawed."

I don't care if he follows or not. I have very distinct ideas about who is a bad guy and I pass up multiple people that he thinks would be fine and I refuse. After fifteen minutes of him pointing out people that I should bite, I am well and truly annoyed with him. "Listen you classist fuck, we are going to," I look around and spot a nice dark area set back where people will forget us, "sit over there and wait. Trust me, I don't mind killing. But I want to kill with some fucking thought behind it."

He looks surprised, but shrugs and follows me over there. We lean against a wall in the shadows. This spot gives us a good view plus, I can hear for a few blocks if I try, which I am now. Another ten minutes of waiting and I hear heavy footsteps moving toward us from the left. From in front of us, I see a teenager running toward us. His back pack flops heavily against his back as he checks his watch and puts on a burst of speed as he rounds the corner, passing us in a cloud of sweat and fear. I can smell the money in his bag, and the drugs. He stops at the corner of the building we are leaning on and the heavy footsteps of a person keep walking toward us. Heavy footsteps comes into view. He is an older white male, looks very well to do.

He walks up to the teenager, snarling at him, "Hand it over." Holding his hand out as the kid slips the backpack off and passes it over.

As the man checks the bag, the kid says, "I couldn't quite get it all sold. My foster mother grounded me after she found the bag. She says I can't do this anymore."

He grabs the kid by the chin, saying, "She doesn't get to say and neither do you. You make sure you get the rest of this sold this week and pick up the drop from the usual spot. If you don't, I'll be by your house personally to take care of that sweet little foster mom of yours. Don't try me."

The kid stammers, "Y-y-yess, sir. I'll get it sold, I promise."

He shoves the kid back from him and grabs the money from the kid's backpack. I smell the kid's intense fear and shame from here and I turn to Mikael, saying, "Catch that boy. Take the drugs, and bring them to me. He, the man, is the one. But I want to leave the drugs with him and maybe they will forget the kid. Tell the kid to come clean to the foster mom and they should move."

Mikael has this amused look on his face as he nods and I watch the kid walking toward us. I can hear heavy footsteps walking back the way he came. I slip past the kid and leave Mikael to deal with him. A brief run and I pass the man, appearing to come out of the shadows of an alley and lean on a wall, with a long, noisy sigh. I lean down to fix my socks, angling so he gets a good view of half my backside. I hear him slow down as I adjust my sock while his heart rate picks up. Good. I straighten and lean against the wall with another dramatic sigh, and he clears his throat. With a pretend jump, I look around and, spotting him, I say, "Oh my, you startled me. I thought you were... someone else. But you look much nicer."

He smiles, predator on the hunt, "Sure is late for a pretty girl like you to be wandering around by yourself. Do you need an escort somewhere? Or a ride?"

I smile widely when he asks if I want a ride. I let my eyes

flick up and down his body, saying, "You know, I could use a ride. Is your car near?"

He is only a couple of feet away from me now. I could rip his throat out now, but I want to wait. Want him to get to his car so I can shove his body in it when I am done. I feel Mikael following us as the man leads me to his car. He hits the button to unlock his car and after he tosses the backpack in the car, he turns to face me, he unfastens his pants and drops them to the ground as he leans against the closed back door, "I thought we could start here," he says as he takes his short, fat cock in his hand to point at me.

I smile and lean in to whisper in his ear, "I think we should start here," I say as I bring my arms up to circle him and keep his arms pinned while I sink my teeth into his neck. He yells but there is no one near to hear him but Mikael and he isn't reporting me. As I feed he weakens and moans, I move my arms so I can grab his with my hands and hold him up. I feel his pelvis thrusting at my leg but there is no strength to it, I just have to hope that he doesn't come on me. His death is imminent, and I release his neck. Mikael says, "Lick the wounds so they'll heal." A swipe of my tongue and they disappear. I ease him into his car seat, lifting his legs and tucking them in. I leave his pants around his ankles, though. Then I take his disgusting face in my hands and he smiles a goofy smile at me as I jerk his head too far and snap his sorry neck. His body stiffens. One last jerk as he dies. I pull his wallet out of his pants and then lean in to check the car for anything else. I find more drugs, great. But also a few fat stacks of money. I take those and turn to Mikael. He hands over the backpack. I look at it and, taking the drugs out, I put them between his legs. Then I shove the wallet and the money in the pack and put it on. I tuck his arm into his lap and kick the door shut.

Looking over at Mikael, I ask, "Ready to go home?"

* * *

The walk back seems a lot shorter, possibly because we aren't meandering about looking for a person to feed on. I get why he felt the need to take me out hunting. He wants to be the big, strong protector. It's nice, but not something I need or want. What I did need was laid, and he filled that need pretty handily. I wonder if he would fill that need again? We get to the house and he is everywhere. He is opening the door for me, hand on my elbow as we go through rooms... I don't know if dick is worth this. Is this because I am a new vampire or because I am a woman?

"Are you always like this with new vampires?"

"What do you mean?"

"I mean, are you worried I will hurt someone or that I will be hurt?"

He scrunches his face a little in thought, "A little of both? You are new and it is a concern that you could go batshit if not fed in a timely manner. At the same time, you are a woman that has ended up under my protection for a variety of reasons, so I am concerned in that way as well."

"I think I can live with that, but could you maybe tone it down? I promise if I feel in danger or like there might be a possibility that I am the danger, I will say something rather than hide it. Can you tone it down, knowing that I will absolutely come to you for help before the problem gets big?"

He eyes me in silence, "I will try but I make my own

judgements and if I think you may slip past the point of no return without realizing it, I will intervene."

"I can live with that." We make it to the kitchen and find all the other vampires in there having a drink. They have mixed a sweet wine with the blood, so we get the sweet taste with the blood. I can't wait to try it. Eason is acting as bartender and he gets Mikael and myself each a glass. I try it and I love it. We spend our last couple hours of the night talking with them in the kitchen. Sunrise draws near and we all get tired. I am the first to say good night to everyone. I am still adjusting and I could use some sleep. Leaving the kitchen alone and feeling like I can finally breathe. The little bit of space is nice and I am looking forward to curling up in that gigantic bed by myself. Before I am half up the stairs, Mikael catches up with me. He walks with me in silence to the bedroom. At the doorway, he asks, "May I sleep with you?"

"That depends. Will you be reading more into this than lovers? Not even monogamous lovers. Just lovers, I may have more of them. I am not willing to limit myself in that way."

"I will not read more into it than you allow. I can promise that."

Eleven

JASMINE

I WAKE up the third night after being changed and I remember everything. The past two nights bits and pieces of my memory would come in and I was seeing Mikael a lot, but very little was good.

Suspicions have been crawling in my mind about why I see him in my memories so much without him being an active participant in those lives. It was a sneaking, shady suspicion that I didn't like, and I definitely don't want to be true.

The memories tonight are slamming into place with the ferocity of a woman betrayed, and I have no choice but to realize that I am that woman. I get out of the bed I am sharing with Mikael. Oh, this motherfucker. Does he know? Does he know who I am? How could he? How could he, all those times? I grab my clothing and throw on a pair of jeans with a crop top. It is too hot outside for more. Throwing on the wide-heeled boots, I pick up my clothing and start shoving it in the backpack we took from the kid. With the money still in the backpack, I should be able to find a cheap place. My needs are drastically reduced at this point.

Mikael wakes up as I walk out the bedroom door. I head for the kitchen, to get some blood bags because I don't know that I will have time to hunt tonight. Mikael makes it into the kitchen before I can open the refrigerator. I stop with my hand on the refrigerator and ask him, "Did you know?"

"Did I know you were her?"

I mock him, "Did I know you were her? Yes! Did you know before you turned me or realize at any point since then that I was her? Did you?"

He looks away, "I realized the day of the night I turned you that it was maybe a possibility."

"How?"

"How is it possible?" He looks genuinely confused, but I don't have sympathy in me right now. I grab two bags of blood out of the fridge and stuff them in the pack.

"How did you realize I might be her, me, that she is me?"

He runs a hand across the back of his neck, saying, "I had a dream. She, you, came to me telling me off. I haven't dreamed of her in the form I met her in for a very long time."

"Do you remember what she was telling you off about? Because I bet I know."

"I believe she might have been a little upset that I didn't find her in all this time."

I slip the backpack on my shoulders, "Might be and a

little are a very polite way to attempt to diminish the absolute rage. I am so beyond angry at you. All that time," I step up close to him so I can yell up at him, "you watched me. Showed up and let me feel you near and then stayed hidden. You chose for me without ever letting me know the choice was there to be made, and you made me utterly miserable while you were at it. I could feel you there! I knew you were watching over me. And I was angry, so angry every time I died and remembered everything. I told the powers that be I don't give a single damn if you find me this time. I better not know it. So, of course, they meddle. They put you in the right place at the exact right time for you to save me from the big bad wolf."

I walk around him and head out of the kitchen, saying, "You can be the big bad protector from a damn distance this time, too. I am not staying here and if you hover around my place too much I will," I stop and turn around to find him directly behind me and just barely stopping in time to avoid running me down, "set some really nasty traps. Just because I don't go around people doesn't mean I don't know people. Don't fucking try me, Mikael. You had your chance to call the shots, and you didn't. You left me there. Every time. I am going to go find myself a place to live and work on my shit. You are on thin fucking ice. Don't try your high-handed bullshit."

"You wait just a moment!" He grabs my arm as I turn and I stop, turning toward him and glaring at him.

He takes his hand off me, saying, "My apologies. You can't just leave. You are under my protection. I can't protect you if you aren't here."

I narrow my eyes at him, saying, "Guess I will take my

chances because I am not staying here. Put your hand on me again and you are coming back with a nub. I will rip it off Mikael. Don't fuck with me."

I walk out the front door as he says, "Fine! I didn't want you here, anyway! You just complicate my nice, simple life!"

It hurts hearing those things, but I will never let him see that. My soul still loves him, even as mad as I am at him. I close the door gently behind me and take off at a brisk walk down the drive. My car is here but it can stay here for a while. If he doesn't like it, he can have it towed.

I feel the guy hanging outside the gates, but I jump over them, anyway. Guess I will pop this blood in my backpack into a cooler because lunch just started following me. I lead him to the downtown area, weaving my way into a more secluded spot. He finally catches up to me. I was beginning to think he wouldn't.

He appears next to me, though I could hear him running up. Sloppy. He says, "Hey baby, remember me?" and flashes his fangs at me.

Raising a brow, I say, "That's it? I put in all this effort to lead you to a nice secluded spot and wait for you to make you move and flashing your fangs is what you have for me? I have been more frightened by drive by dick pics." Putting my hands on his chest and smiling at him as I gently push him up against a building, "You should be more creative. Remember that honey brings the bees in while shit only brings flies," I am whispering all this in his ear and this guy is so hard up that he is dry humping my leg double time, he cums as I sink my fangs into his neck, his body thrusting hard a few times as he ejaculates his last. He is so relaxed he never realizes that I have all but drained him dry. I lick the holes in his neck to close them and lower him to the ground. I wonder if it is true that they, um, we turn to dust if we are stabbed in the heart? Walking around, I find a discarded chunk of pipe and I bring it back over to the body. Ew, does not look good. Very dried corpse going on here. I impale him with the pipe, and he puffs into a disgusting cloud of dust.

Oh god, I've got fuck-boy in my nose.

Note to self: watch out for the dust cloud. I dust myself off as best I can. I head for this shady ass trailer park a friend of mine used to live in. The manager was always up partying and that was always the best time to catch him and rent a place.

Getting there was quicker than I thought. Or maybe I don't account for how fast I can walk now. I slip the backpack off, grab some cash to shove in a pocket, and hang it in a tree before I go up to the trailer that is obviously having a party. My friend lived here for two years and it wasn't the safest place, but it was cheap and the owner mostly left her alone.

I walk up to the party and someone hands me a drink. I ask where Jack is and they yell over the music, "I think he's out back shagging some chick."

I nod my thanks and wander around to the back porch area. Yup, there he is, bumping uglies with some woman. I turn my back to them and wait for him to finish. It would be a much longer wait if I tried to wait for her to get there. I'd probably have to go do it myself. He certainly is not getting her there. Oh finally, he finished. Did he really ask her if it was good for her? Jeez, you couldn't tell, man? She was bored. Not my business. Not my business at all. I wait till they both have their clothes adjusted and are having a smoke. I walk up loudly so they won't guess I was waiting for them to finish.

"Hi, I was told you were the guy in charge here?"

He peers at me through the darkness and the haze of drugs and alcohol floating in his system. Fuck, he smells more chemical than organic now. I step into the light so he can see me and he smiles, "Oh, yeah. That's me. What do you need? Something wrong with your place?"

"Well, I need a place. Do you have any open?"

"Oooh! Yeah, yeah I fuckin' do! Hold on, let me get the keys."

He hops up and walks in the house like he isn't on a massive amount of drugs and I am just amazed at the human body. He comes back with a flashlight and some keys and tells the woman he just fucked, "Hey thanks, I'll catch up with you later. I got to tend the business side of things." He waves at her as he walks on down the stairs. I follow him because I don't care about her and he starts talking, telling me, "Ok, so the place, its got one bedroom with a big ass bathroom and all the usual stuff, kitchen that has things. If something breaks and it bothers you, let me know I'll send someone to fix it. Rent is five fifty a month, but it includes everything. No pets, no kids. This neighborhood isn't good for either of those." He walks up to a small trailer, flips through keys and picking one, unlocks the door. He opens it and steps back, holding the door and saying, "Go ahead and check it out. I'll wait out here. Uh, did you have a baking accident or something?" He asks as he uses a finger to point, indicating the dust I have covering me.

"Yeah, sometimes I help a friend with her baking business. Tonight an experimental cake exploded."

I hear the snick of a lighter as he lights himself a cigarette while he waits. He was accurate in his description. It is not the worst place I have ever lived and I think it may be better than some of them. At the very least, I will be a lot safer, considering my current abilities. I walk back out and pull some cash out of my pocket, telling him, "I'll take it."

"Great, five fifty and it is yours for one month. It will continue to be yours contingent upon you paying rent in a timely manner. I don't care about reasons, I just want rent. I don't want to fuck around chasing you for it."

I peel off six one hundred-dollar bills and hand them over to him. He hands me a set of keys as he says, "I don't have change."

I tell him don't worry about it. He says cool and starts to walk off but turns around, "Say, you wouldn't happen to be a dealer, would you?"

"No, sorry."

"Well, that's a shame. Would have been convenient. Have a good night. I know I will."

I chuckle and retrieve my backpack from the tree before going into my new place and putting the blood in the fridge.

* * *

Mikael

· · ·

"I can't believe she would walk away from safety and better accommodations than she ever had just because she is mad at me."

Eason and Sebastian share a look. Sebastian shrugs and looks at me, saying, "Mikael, care to explain what exactly you mean? Who left and, more importantly, why are they mad at you?"

I pace the length of the library, telling them, "Jasmine. Jasmine is mad at me because she's my dead wife."

Scarlett says, "What do you mean, she is your dead wife? Did you kill her?"

I shoot her a glare, "No, I didn't kill her. She is the latest incarnation of my wife. When she got all her memories back, she remembered and she was not pleased that I had been making choices about her life all that time."

Scarlett laughs, and my glare intensifies. "Look, I did what was best for her. She had happy lives and how was I to know that she could tell I was watching over her? I had no idea. There was no way I could know that. It wouldn't have changed much, anyway."

Scarlett stops laughing, saying, "And that is what she is mad about. You did what was best for her without consulting her. What you did wasn't best for her. Have you even asked her what her previous lives were like?" She crosses her arms over her chest, "I know good and well you didn't. You couldn't have heard her story and still managed to wrap yourself around thinking you are the injured party here."

"Is that so? Well, why don't you share with me? Why shouldn't I make decisions about what is best for her based on what you know?" I lean against a bookcase. I'm confident in my choices.

She shakes her head at me, saying, "Oh no, I am not telling another vampire's story without their permission. If you want to know what of her story she told me, you should ask her about her lives without you. She didn't tell you because you are not ready to treat her like a person. A perfectly capable adult human being. You don't even know how old she is right now, do you?"

"Of course I do! She's..."

"Not been asked what her age is by you. Because you considered her some sort of weird child."

The smug look on Scarlett's face just pisses me off. More because she isn't wrong. "You might be right. If you were, what would you suggest I do?"

Scarlett snorts at me, "If. Men." She stands and Chloe stands with her. She says, "I suggest you change the way you treat her and perhaps take an interest in her as a person."

The two women leave the library. I stand there thinking about things and when I look up, I am alone once again, Eason and Sebastian having left as well.

* * *

Chloe

Scarlett drags me directly to the kitchen as soon as we clear the library door. Soon as we walk through the swinging door, she pulls out her phone and taps the screen. Music blares from her phone as she sets it down on the counter and walks across the kitchen to the side farthest away from the doorway to the rest of the house. I follow her because obviously she wants to talk in private. She settles herself with her back to the wall where she can see the door to the kitchen while lean against the countertop and ask quietly, "So what's on your mind?"

"I think you should go check on Jasmine. You wisely said nothing back there, so if you take off out the back door here, he will never notice. I need to stick around and be angry, mouthy. Seen and distracting."

I jump when Eason agrees. "Sorry Chloe. I thought you saw me when Scarlett did. You are the only one that was silent and I can cover for you, saying you are in my bed. I am going up there shortly, anyway. I'll leave my window open and you can come in that way."

I look between the two of them, saying, "Makes it a lot easier having you guys behind what I was planning to do. The only thing I want to do differently is to go out your window as well. Be easier for you to say I am up there if I go up there with you."

Scarlett nods, "Excellent. Go. Both of you. I'll bring a couple glasses of wine up and drop them off with you in a few Eason. Chloe, make sure she knows we are there for her, even if he is not part of her life. I like her little scrappy attitude."

"Me too. Come on E, let's walk sexy up the stairs."

He grins at me, saying, "Walk sexy? Should I give my hips that extra sway or shall I use a fireman's carry to get you up their smacking that ass the entire way?"

"Go for the sway, lover boy. We'll talk about the

spanking when I get back."

* * *

Ten minutes later, I am out the window and walking around to the driveway. I check on her car and it is still here, so she took off walking. Excellent, so much easier to track her that way. Hopping the fence and I can smell the direction she went, but I smell someone else on her trail. Following her and her stalker to a less occupied area of downtown and I see the pipe she put through her assailant still sticking out of the ground. I can't tell if she was that mad or just accidentally pushed harder than she meant to push. Kicking it over and following her scent out of the area, I come to a trailer park and she seems to have gone there. Looks like a party happening in that first trailer. Maybe I could grab a snack. No, focus. Find Jasmine, not snackies. Still following her trail, and I am led to a trailer a few back. I can smell her in there, so I knock. I hear her walk to the door and see her peer out at me before she opens the door, exclaiming, "Chloe! How did you find me so fast?"

"Well, you have a distinctive scent and vampires have a great sense of smell. Are you going to invite me in?"

"Oh, yes! Sorry, I was just so surprised to see you. Come in, come in." She backs up and I come up the stairs, closing the door behind me.

"No furniture yet, so you'll have to deal with the floor if you want to sit." She sits then and leans against a wall, so I do the same.

"I followed your whole trail. Who was the vampire that

followed you from the house?"

"It was one of the guys that murdered everyone in the last trailer park I lived in. They were kind of the spark that started all this."

"Oh. So they know you are with Mikael."

"It looks like it. But unless they had backup that didn't get close enough for me to smell them or hear them, they don't know I'm not there just yet. It horrified me when he turned into a puff of fuck boy dust, got it up my nose. Yuck."

I laugh at the picture of her stabbing him and getting the dust in her nose. "So what are you planning to do, beyond not come back to the house for now? Because I am not here to talk you back, we were all concerned for you."

"We?"

"Yeah, Scarlett, Eason, and Sebastian. Me too, of course. I just figured that was obvious since I am here."

"Thanks, I didn't expect that. I mean, you all have known him a lot longer. So far, I have to find a job soon and I need to buy some things to get by here. Thinking I might try dancing."

"Girl, that is a great idea. Plus, as long as you are careful, you can feed from the ones that pay for private dances. Little from this one, little from that one, and by the end of the night you have had plenty to go home happily sated. Plus, being a vampire, you don't have to worry that you will wear out your knees or your back. Live cheap and invest. You are in a great position to raise your circumstances drastically. Financial independence will never go out of style."

"That is along the lines of what I was thinking. I just wasn't sure about it. I don't have the confidence yet that comes with being a vampire for so long. And I could only wish for the confidence of a mediocre white man. But I am working on it, getting my crown on straight, so to speak."

"Good. Now, you know Mikael is going to find you, right?"

"Yeah, I know." She rolls her eyes. "He is so frustrating! And maddening. Why would he leave me there all those times? Fucking asshole. Who is he to decide what is best for me? Without even talking to me or getting to know my situation? I may still have sex with him, sometimes, because that was good. But I am not committing to him and I am very likely to sleep around with some other people too. He is just going to have to get right with that. And if he wants something more far in the future, I'll think about it. Far in the future when that time comes."

"Ha! Good. Make him work for it. He's played martyred-know-it-all for entirely too long and it will be glorious to watch you wake him up. We all tried, but we aren't the one he has been chasing all this time and didn't have half the effect you have. Not to say we expect you to fix him. My opinion there is based on what you said, nothing more."

We talk a little longer till I feel sunrise on its way. We say our goodbyes and I head for Morhall.

Twelve

JASMINE

IT HAS BEEN a week since I left Mikael's Morhall house. Tonight was night two of my new job as an exotic dancer. Being a vampire is a tremendous benefit in this. I was able to pick up the moves and practice for a few days without injuring myself. Getting access to a pole was the most troublesome part. Trailers aren't built for that. I make plenty to make it worth being there four nights a week. The girls are mostly nice, though there appear to be a couple of Karens in the mix.

Mostly, I love it because I am free. Free of anyone else's wants or needs. The lap dances really are a buffet for me. Hypnotize them a little with my tits, and if they notice me biting them, they don't care. I never leave a mark and I feed sparingly from any one patron. If they turn into stalkers, hmm, I will get a full meal all at once. I almost hope for a couple of stalkers. In the meantime, though, I hear the pitter-patter of a vampire following me. A clumsy, idiot vampire with less sense than his boss gave him credit for. Of course, his boss can't have that much sense if he really sent another flunky to die.

Happily, I don't even have to hunt for a broken pipe this time. I have a bowie knife strapped to my thigh. It does mean I have to lure this idiot somewhere... Ugh! Ok, there is a reasonably quiet area about two blocks from here. I head for that. Walking just a little faster so he realizes I know he is back there, but will probably think I am just afraid. I love it when I can surprise them. Wish they would make it more difficult, though.

I get to the area and slow down to search the shadows, like I am seeking a door. He catches up and grabs my upper arms, shoving me against a wall as he says, "Hello little bunny, let's you and me take a little walk."

I smile up at him, the knife in my hand already, saying, "Oh, but I thought we were going to play a much more fun game now?" I slip my arms up around him and I press my body against his. He freezes as I rub my body against him and then starts to melt, putty in my hands. Kissing my way up his chest and right to the artery pulsing so sweetly in his neck. I bite him and he tries to jerk away, but my arms are locked around him. I feed, pulling hard from the vein. He is quickly weakened, and I lower him gently to the ground as I drain nearly everything from him. I release him and lick my lips, tasty. With a lick, the two little piercing holes and watch them heal, just in case this one doesn't poof. I grab the neckline of my shirt and put it over my mouth and nose before I stab him in case he goes poof.

I plunge the blade through his chest and poof. Only a cloud of ashes left of him. Wiping my blade clean, and noticing that I broke the tip. I need to gauge the stab better. Oh well, I will keep using this for now. I don't want to waste money on replacing knives until I am better at not burying them in the pavement below.

Pulling my shirt back in place, I dust myself off. I need to carry a lint roller or something. These dusty fuckers cling. Why does the dust always go up my nose? Yuck!

The walk home is going to take longer, but that's fine. I found out while I was practicing; the sunlight doesn't affect me any more than it does Mikael. I haven't checked yet to see if I can do any magic tricks. I don't know if Mikael will be willing to teach me any of what he knows. At some point I will need to ask him, but things have been so quiet and just nice, I haven't wanted to upset the balance. And if I am really honest, I just haven't wanted to show any sign of weakness to a man that wants to own me. I feel like letting him have any kind of upper hand would be a mistake at this point.

Walking up the drive of the trailer park, I see a familiar someone sitting at the door of my trailer. Well, I guess this works out to some extent. He came to find me and that tips the balance in my favor by his reckoning. Maybe I can ask him about the magic.

He stands as I draw closer, saying, "What the hell are you doing out so late? You know sunrise is in just a little while! You are a newborn vamp, much more sensitive to the effects of the sun!"

"That is the first thing you want to say when you see me after I have been gone for over a week? That's what you want to lead with?"

"Shit. I'm sorry. No, it isn't. I was worried about you."

"Well, fortunately for me. I inherited your ability to be out in the bright sunlight with no ill effects."

"May I ask what is the dust all over you?"

I look down at my shirt and hands, "Ugh, it's fuck boy dust. Some vampire was following me and planning to take me to that guy. I didn't want to go, so I took him out. Did you know vampires poof into a disgusting cloud of dust? Because they certainly fucking do. And it sticks. I hate it. FYI, never get fuck boy dust up your nose, it takes forever to get that out. Even with a neti pot."

"I... What? Fuck boy? Have you killed more than one? Why didn't you come to me?"

"If you want to continue to question me, you are going to have to do it while I shower. I am covered in fuck boy dust. Move so I can get in the trailer. You can talk to me while I shower. It isn't like you've never seen me naked."

Thirteen

JASMINE

AFTER HE MOVES, I lead the way into the trailer. He looks mildly horrified by the place and I am entertained by that even as it pricks at the shame I have held for so long over being trailer trash. I get to the bathroom and start the water going while I strip down. He comes in and leans against the sink while I wait for the water to heat.

"Good grief, you're sexy even when covered in dust. Get in so I can think."

With a grin, I say, "I like it better when you don't, but the water is warm enough now, so you are in luck." I get in the shower and start soaping up everything. I feel a genuine need to scrub away the fuck boy.

Mikael is silent for a bit. When he speaks, the first thing he says is, "What I meant to lead with is, will you please come back? I hate that you are mad at me."

"I hate to break it to you, but me coming back there will not make me less mad at you. It will just mean that you are frequently in my line of fire. And I assure you, I have plenty of things to yell at you about. I need time by myself. Because the shit you did is not all I am dealing with, you know that, right?"

"Erm, admittedly, I don't know as much as I would like to know about you. Would you maybe be willing to tell me about you?"

"I might. But it is going to be slowly. You want to get to know me, do it the way any other one-night stand would have to, drop by. Take me out. Be my friend. I am damaged goods, baby," I say as I turn the water off, "and I refuse to jump into a relationship because you want to be in one. Hand me the towel."

I open the curtain and he is holding the towel out to me while his eyes feast on my body. My lips pick up on one side in a half smile. "Sir, my eyes are up here."

He laughs, "Sorry. I haven't really had sex except you. You are distracting."

"What? Not at all? Seriously?"

"I mean, I have had some one-night stands, but they were just need, I only did it when I couldn't stand it any longer."

"Good grief, my dude, no one can say you aren't dedicated. We can have sex if you like. I know I wouldn't mind being thoroughly railed. But, still going to insist that you go home and I refuse to come back to live at Morhall right now."

"I, uh, I think I would really like that. But um, I think I could spend a day doing dirty things to you. Would that be a problem?"

"I have no problem with a day of sex. And, I have been

wondering, do vampires exchange blood when they have sex? I haven't had vamp on vamp sex yet, so is that a thing?"

He shrugs, saying, "It depends on the vampires. We can try it out if you like?"

"I thought you'd never ask," I say as I drop my towel and step out of the shower.

* * *

Leonidas

Stuck under this trailer is not how I wanted to spend my day, but for the first time in years, I missed the time to get back home before the sun rose by accident. I watched from the shadows as she killed one of my goons. It was the sexiest thing I have ever seen. She seduced him into letting her close and the entire time had her knife in her hand, waiting for the moment to strike. Lethal and curvy, god what a woman. Horrible that the idiot that saved her the first time I saw her was the one to turn her. I wonder if he told her about the way turning someone allows you to track them and feel their emotions? Probably not judging by what I heard tonight. How did neither of them smell me? Wait, she said she had fuck boy dust up her nose. That would explain why she didn't, but he should have smelled me on the breeze. Perhaps he stayed to stake his claim. Not that it will do any good. I always get what I want and I want her more than anything. She and I, we, could rule our own little corner of the world together.

The trailer above me shudders on its pilings and I eye it, this place was not meant for vampire sex. I hope they don't bring the place down on me. Her cries of pleasure are driving me to distraction, but the sun has me trapped till this evening. Why isn't she at his place? He wants her there, but she specifically said that would not happen. What did he do? How can I exploit that to make her mine? I need to change what my goons are doing. Get one of the girls to go to work at the same club. I need information.

I stretch and slip my hands under my head and close my eyes. She is quiet for a moment. Maybe I can get to sleep.

Fourteen

JASMINE

THE CLUB IS KICKING TONIGHT, but Club Amnesia is kicking most nights. Especially now that there are two vampires working here. Surreal performances are a thing and these humans are eating it up. Maybe I should buy this place? If I can save and invest just right... This could be really lucrative and I could turn it into a haven for the supernatural. I have to put that thought in the back of my mind as Mila finishes her set. I watch as she collects her money. The guys love her. She is pretty fantastic and I like her. Which is causing me some conflict, because she works for the guy that has been trying to catch me. His name is Leonidas, which I only know because she told me. Mikael has not given up any information yet. Beyond that, he wants me. And wants me to come home. Ugh. No chance.

She told me the first night I met her she works for him and that she came here to get a job because he told her to for information on me. She also repeated a message he sent to me, telling me that he has ordered everyone to protect me as opposed to killing me, and that it thrilled him to see I had become one of them. I still don't know what to think about that, but Mila just walked past and my intro music is on. I strut out on to the stage and they start hooting and hollering. Halfway through my set, I feel eyes on me, more than the usual from the patrons. I scan the crowd as I move in a slow circle on the pole. Leonidas! He is in a dark corner of the club. His eyes reflect the light back at me as he watches me dance. He meets my eyes and tips his head to me. Fuck. He still looks like danger. He is the definition of the guy momma told me to stay away from. Did momma know trouble would come wrapped in such a sexy package with a voice to make people beg for his bidding? If she did, why didn't she tell me how to stay away when they won't leave you alone?

After I finish my set while trying to keep my eyes from seeking the corner Leonidas is squatting in, he doesn't need to know I want to see more of him. I loiter in the dressing room after I finish changing into my street clothes. As I watched Mila leave earlier, laughing, I asked what she was laughing at and she said, "You, chickenshit."

I rolled my eyes at her, but she isn't wrong. The house mom is eyeballing me. If I don't get my ass gone, she is going to ask questions. Sigh. I get up and sling my backpack over my shoulders, deep breath, and I head for the outside world. I get half a block away and he steps out of the shadows.

Leonidas. His dark skin gleams in the streetlights, but his eyes catch me. Hold me hostage. Deep pools of secrets that I want to unravel.

He breaks the spell, saying, "I watched you the other night."

"The same way you watched me tonight? Enjoy the show?"

A growl comes from him that sends a shiver over my skin and directly to my core. "No, though the show tonight... I would love a private showing. No, I watched you when my guy Brent found you."

"Oh. You saw that."

"Mmm, I did. It was stunning. I love dangerous creatures. May I walk you home?"

"You love dangerous creatures? Is that why you called off your goons and sent Mila to get information?"

"Partly. Mostly, as a vampire, you stand to lose as much as I do if you were to play witness to the authorities. I would have continued had I not seen you in action last night."

"Ah. I see. So my life matters when your cock is doing the thinking. Well, color me surprised. Walk me home if you want. I can't stop you from walking in the same direction. I will knock the stupid out of you if you try anything."

He chuckles and I think my panties are wet now. "I promise I will keep my hands to myself until you ask me to put them on you. You will eventually ask, but I have time."

"Really? Morals in a guy that fancies himself the leader of a vampire gang? How did that happen?"

"Make no mistake, my morals, as you call them, extend only so far. I have no problem killing and stealing is not an issue for me. I protect what is mine and I take what I need."

"Ah, so you don't force sex?"

"No. That is the one line. Torture is on the table, but rape is not."

"That is an interesting set of morals. Can't say I am not happy about the last part though. So why? Why that one line?"

"None of your business."

"Oh, you get to send people to collect information and to kill me, but I don't get the answers to questions about your morals? I see."

He snarls at me and I laugh at him, "I could still decide to kill you."

"If you're feeling froggy, then jump, big man. We'll see what we see, won't we?"

He laughs, saying, "You are the most insane woman I have ever met. I think I love you. Fine. My mother conceived me from a rape. It, it messed her up. She had a lot of problems. I saw people robbed, beaten, tortured, and people that somehow didn't die after someone tried to murder them. None of them had the problems she did or even close. I found out a lot more of her history from her friends after I was grown. I never want to do that to someone."

"I'm sorry about your mom. My parents are dead. They died when I was younger. Thank you for sharing that with me."

"You're welcome. So what's a guy got to do to get a date with an exotic dancer?"

Mikael rounds a corner, and seeing Leonidas with me, he speeds over to stand between us. Growling at Leonidas, he shoves me behind him, saying, "What are you doing here, Leonidas? I told you to stay away from her."

Fucking shit, what is it with growling that turns me on? How fucked up am I? Leonidas laughs at him, saying, "Put away your sword and shield, pretty boy. I'm walking her home. I called my guys off now that I know she is one of us. Why didn't you tell me that, in one of your little messages? Hmm?"

"It was none of your business."

Leonidas smiles cruelly, "Oh, but I think I might make it my business. What else are you keeping quiet? Did you tell her everything about the bond between the maker and the one turned? Did you tell her you were in contact with me the day you took her away or that you knew who I was to begin with?"

"I told her what she needed to know. She had enough on her mind already. But you, you stay away from her. I know what kind of shady dealings you take part in. She wants no part of it. I claimed her. She is mine."

Leonidas takes a deep breath, saying, "Odd, it would seem your claim has not been accepted, as I cannot smell it. Seems like Jasmine here is still a free agent. Jasmine, what would you like me to do?"

I am still glaring daggers at Mikael after all I heard, saying, "I want you to leave for now. There are some things I want to discuss with Mikael here." Leonidas' face falls just a fraction, and he turns away as he nods. I continue, saying, "And I am off on Monday. What time will you be picking me up for our date?"

The faces on these two when I dropped that bomb, priceless. Leonidas' sly smile and Mikael's shock. I could live a thousand years and never get so perfect a set of reactions.

Leonidas says, "I'll see you at ten." A small wave and he disappears into the shadows.

* * *

"How long have you known Leonidas?" I ask as I start walking.

"Are you really going to go out with him?"

"I said I am. I have no intention of ghosting him. How long have you known him?"

"I'm really not comfortable with the idea of you going out with him."

"That's nice. Are you going to answer my question or," I stop walking and turn to face him, "am I saying good night to you now?"

Mikael sighs, saying, "I will answer your question. I've known him for the last thirty years or so. We have maintained casual contact since we met. We move in different circles for the most part. He is useful for the occasional odd job I need done that skirts legality."

"So you keep in contact with him because he is good for the times you don't want to get your hands dirty? Wonderful." I start walking again, "What haven't you told me about the bond between us? The one from you turning me. Not the one from our previous relationship."

"Heerrmm, um, that one. You may not like it so much. And that's why I didn't tell you about it. I knew it would just make you more mad than you already were when your memories came in. But I promise I haven't been using it though. I found you by scent."

"What does it do, Mikael?"

"It allows me to track you and know your emotions. But the effect wears off over time."

"I see. And does this happen faster if they are separated?"

"No. Time or death are the only ways to end it. But I can promise not to use it if you aren't in trouble."

"How are you going to know I am in trouble if you aren't using it?" He pales and I know I've caught him red-handed. "How would you know, Mikael?"

"I would hope that you would call me."

"Have you ever given me your phone number?"

"Maybe?" He shrugs, "I really have not been using it, I promise. Not like all the time. Just occasionally to check in on you. I monitored you the night you left." He looks away, saying, "Just to be sure."

I narrow my eyes and keep walking. I wonder... "You can feel whatever I feel? When you choose?"

"Yes. Generally one would try not to be invasive, closing it off when it appears the student needs privacy."

"Meaning that if I have sex, you will feel it?"

"Theoretically, yes."

"Ok. You haven't once used that while you and I were having sex?"

His mouth falls open, and he grimaces, saying, "Um, no. I don't want to feel your emotions while we have sex. Having your stuff in me while we... no. That would be weird."

"So you wouldn't want to feel it when you do something and I am really into it? That wouldn't turn you on? Really? Because I am kind of turned on thinking about it. I almost want to turn someone just for the experience."

Mikael jumps in front of me, causing me to slam into him. He catches me before I fall and says, "You can't turn anyone! Not ever! We can't risk the magic in my blood and, most likely, yours, manifesting in others."

I step out of his arms and rub my nose, grumbling, "You have got to calm down. Do you realize you could have just said that instead of being a dramatic ass? Do you think that applies to exchanging blood with another vampire? I mean, if I were to have sex with," I slant a glance at his face, "say Chloe, and we exchange blood. Will she somehow get powers or is it limited to only those that one of us creates?"

His eyes get wide as he processes what I said. "I don't know. Better to be safe than sorry. You should refrain from allowing other vampires to drink your blood." He shakes his head, saying, "The magic is not finite, as I have had it for a long time. My magic has not been diminished by what you gained and—"

"Wait, you said by what I gained. So I definitely got powers when you turned me? How do you know? How long have you known?" The driveway to my trailer park is just ahead and I walk a little faster. I am so ready to be home. In my space. What is Mikael's malfunction that he thinks he should decide what information I do or do not get?

He looks down as he says, "As soon as you were fully turned."

"So you have known all this time," I stop to turn and face him, "all this time and you continually made it sound like it was just a possibility. What do you think it helps when you keep these things from me? Do you think it makes me feel more charitable toward you? Like you are some big, strong protector because you lie by omission regularly, and sometimes just outright lie. That's not how this works. That's not how any of this works. You don't get to decide what I know or don't know and continue to be in my bed or even a part of my life." I start walking again and he takes a minute to get over himself and catch up.

When he does, he says, "I'm sorry. I keep expecting our relationship to be like it was the first time. I forget that this is a different time and place. That you are a different person with a unique background I know nothing about, even if at your core you are still the woman that I married so very long ago. Please don't give up on me, I promise I will change. I will be the man you need me to be and stop living in a past that you barely recall." He puts his hand on my shoulder and I stop walking to look at him as he says, "I need you to stay in my life, Jasmine. I promise I'll be better."

He looks very sincere. And I feel very certain this is a trap. He sounds like every other guy that doesn't care enough to get his act together, but wants to continue reaping the benefits of a woman in his life. "Fine. But your ass is on probation. I find out you are keeping things from me again and you are out. I loved you once upon a time. And I guess in some small way I still do. But I would walk through fire rather than be continually mistreated by a man ever again."

He nods, "Thank you. I promise I won't keep things that concern you from you." We get to my front door and he says, "Are you going to invite me in today?"

"No Mikael, I need to think. One more question before you go. The powers I got from you. Are you going to teach me how to use them?"

He tugs at his collar, saying, "I don't know. They taught

me that if women know magic, they would do only evil with it. It is... difficult for me to let go of that when I also believe that using magic is against the laws of nature."

"Vampires are against the laws of nature. Dead creatures with their souls trapped in reanimated bodies who must feed from the blood of others in order to survive."

He scowls, saying, "I know, I know. But we have no choice in being vampires. We have a choice about the magic. We don't have to use it and we don't have to let it spread beyond ourselves. Honestly, I have only ever made three vampires, counting you. I never thought it was a great idea."

Smirking at him, I ask, "I know how you made me by accident. Is that how you made the other two? In the uh, heat of the moment, so to speak?"

"What? Oh," he runs a hand across the back of his neck, looking down he says, "no. They petitioned me to turn them. They were men of power and they had served their terms, made their money and done service. But they still had not lived. They hadn't wandered and enjoyed the money they had accumulated. They were unattached, had no family to speak of, and they simply wished to quietly disappear with plenty of time to continue living. We all died much younger most of the time back then. It seemed very reasonable, and I granted it to them."

"Wow. Ok. Well, I need to get inside and you need to go home. Daylight is coming and I at least want to continue to seem like it would affect me."

"A kiss before I go?"

Sigh, "Not today Mikael, not today." I pull the door to the trailer open and step in, shutting it behind me. I don't hear him walk away, but I would be more surprised if I did.

Laying face down in the middle of the living room floor is all I can manage right now. This is ridiculous. The audacity of the man is stunning in its scope. I roll over and sit up. I have a date! Fuck, I almost forgot. I have a date with Leonidas on Monday. I can't remember the last time I went out on a date. Good grief, his voice. How am I going to go an entire evening listening to that voice and not have my wicked way with him? Fuck. Where is he taking me? It's not like we can go out to eat... Well we can, but that is not a dine in kind of experience. What should I wear? Maybe he will come by the club tonight and I can ask him.

I fall back to laying down. Being a new vampire is hard. Shit.

Fifteen

JASMINE

LEONIDAS ARRIVES JUST a little before ten. I
have put on the makeup, but I haven't dressed yet because I
didn't know what we were going to do. I open the door and
invite him in, telling him, "I haven't changed yet because I
wasn't sure where we were going. Beyond being pretty
certain that you would not be taking me to dinner in a
restaurant."

He laughs, "No. No restaurants, they get suspicious if
you don't eat the food you ordered. We are going to a few
places, if you are game. But I do have one stop to make
before we officially go to the places I have planned. I
brought a cooler with blood, so you don't have to worry
about going hungry away from people."

"Ok, a little mystery, but you are bringing food. I like it.
Give me five minutes."

I disappear into the bedroom. Throwing on the
stretchy black jeans and fitted black tank, a sparkly black

bolero jacket, and my chunky heeled boots to finish the outfit off. I check myself in the mirror, adding a scrunchy to my wrist as I left my hair flowing freely tonight. The tank's v displays my boobs nicely and the stretchy jeans hug my ass like a second skin while still allowing for movement.

I walk out to the living room and Leonidas lets out a low whistle, "Pretty lady, you sure know how to wrap a package. Ready?"

I laugh, "Thanks. Yes, I am."

Leonidas leads the way, and I shut and lock the trailer on my way out. It won't stop anyone, but it might give them pause. I turn and he is standing next to an older model Chevy pickup. I walk around it admiring the work he has put into keeping or restoring it to such good condition. He is holding the passenger door open for me. Grinning, he says, "Like what you see?"

I nod, getting in as I say, "I do. Is this original or restored?"

"Restored. I found her in terrible shape a few years back and spent my spare time working on her." He closes the door and walks around the truck, getting into the driver's seat. He starts the truck and grips the steering wheel, saying, "When we set the day for this date, I wasn't thinking about my usual Monday night date." I raise a brow but remain silent so he can continue on. "I visit my mom every Monday night. It was arranged with the home that I would be an exception, so that I could visit her because, well, day visits are out of the question. I am telling you all this because that is where I need to go. I can't do it on a different night. You can come in with me or wait outside, as you please. If that is, you still want to go?"

"I do actually. And I would like to come in. I am curious to meet your mother."

He exhales in a rush of air, saying, "Ok. Ok." He puts the truck in reverse and backs out of my drive into the shared one before putting it in drive and heading toward the nursing home. "My mom, she isn't always all there anymore. While I tell everyone I am fifty years old, I was actually thirty-five when I was turned and it has been fifty years since then. But I feel like the life before this didn't entirely count. My mom, though, she had me younger than was good for her. So, between that and her being long-lived in general, she is a hundred years old. She is relatively spry for her age. But her mind, that was slipping in and out of time long before she needed to be in a home. If she says something strange, don't worry about it. She does it a lot."

"No problem. I am honored that you will let me meet her or know where she is at all."

"Yeah. You are the only person who I have brought here. Ever. So don't tell anyone, right?"

"I won't. Even if we don't remain friends, your mom is off limits."

He pulls into the parking lot of a posh nursing home. This place looks like it could be a fancy country club. He leads the way, pushing a button near the front door to be allowed entrance. The nurse at the desk nods a greeting, saying, "She's been really quiet lately. All there, but silent. It's a little spooky."

"Thanks Judy. Maybe she'll open up while I'm here." I walk with him through a labyrinth of halls to a room marked A. Manoie. He knocks lightly on the door and we hear a voice answer softly from the other side, bidding him to enter. He opens the door and walks in. I follow behind him.

As he leans in to hug her, she says, "I always know when it's you. I'm so glad to see you. I have things to tell you. Who is this lovely woman?" She grabs his face and peers into his eyes, saying, "Must be terribly serious for you to bring her by here. You never bring anyone to see me."

"I don't run with a good crowd mom, I can't bring them by to meet you. She is Jasmine."

I wave, "It's very nice to meet you."

His mother pales, "So that's why I kept seeing you wreathed in flowers." Leonidas looks sharply at his mom as she continues, "I have to come clean with you Leonidas. I haven't alway been honest with you and I am dying."

He scoffs, "You'll live to be a hundred and thirty at least."

She shakes her head no, saying, "I'm sorry, my boy, but that isn't the case. I don't have very long left and I need you both to listen. I did not know I would get to meet the woman and I couldn't see her face clearly, but the flowers and the scent, that was very clear." She takes his face in her hands, whispering, "My sweet boy, I am so sorry I couldn't be a better mother when you were younger. I had problems that just wouldn't go away. For all that, I never told you why he did what he did."

Leonidas straightens, his hip resting on the bed, "You don't have to tell me that, mom. It's ok. And he is dead and gone. He can't hurt anyone anymore." The glint in his eyes tells me that Leonidas probably had more than a little to do with him being gone.

His mother nods, "I know. I know he is gone, and I

know you are the reason he is gone. I know he paid for all his sins before you let him leave this earth and I confess, I wasn't unhappy to see it. But you still need to know. He thought, as so many others do, that to violently take the maidenhead of a seer is to take their powers. Men always think that a woman's power lies in her remaining a virgin. Makes me think they know how awful they are to lie with, but that's not here or there. I didn't lose the ability to see because he raped me many times. I lost my sanity. Sanity is, for me, like gossamer threads on the wind. I can't always keep hold of them, so things get out of sorts. Pass me my water, please." Leonidas hands her the water from the table next to her bed and she sips it. Handing it back, she waves me over, saying, "Sit on this other side, dear. I don't take up so much space these days and this is about you, too." I walk over and have a seat. "Good, good. I can't always find all the pieces, but they are here so far. The visions I have had lately, they comfort me greatly. I like knowing that when I am gone, things will change for the better. Who knows, if I get recycled I might even get to live it. Sorry, sorry, I get so side-tracked when I am all here and have someone to talk to."

Leonidas hands her the water again, and she sips it. Handing it back, she points at me, saying, "She is going to change the world. For good or for ill remains to be seen, but she will bring the changes that must happen. If she dies, the world will continue its descent into darkness." She looks directly at me, whispering, "He doesn't know that you took nearly all his power. It was never meant to be his, nor was it meant to belong to the man before him that did the stealing. They were only ever vessels to get the power to you. You must learn how to use it, and you must choose. Your time grows short, the choice will be made for you if you keep dithering about." I sit there doing my best imitation of a fish out of water while she turns back to Leonidas, saying, "You must choose, too. I know you have been running with a dangerous crowd, but they are bad because you let them. Be the leader you were meant to be. The world will be better for it." She takes the glass Leonidas offers her and sips more water. Holding on to it this time, she says, "I don't want to say too much. Just try to remember lies don't benefit anyone and some secrets are to be expected." She looks me in the eye, saying, "Sometimes evil looks like a nice, upstanding guy. Be mindful that people are not always who they appear to be and that what you remember may not be the complete picture."

I nod, telling her, "I will try to be mindful."

She reaches out and grabs my hand, saying, "Not try. You must be mindful. The fate of the world depends on you. It will be another thousand years of darkness if you fail."

She releases my hand and sips her water before handing it over to Leonidas. She leans back on her pillows, saying, "All this seeing I have been doing all week has been exhausting. Jasmine, I need to talk to my boy before he takes you off on your date. Would you be so kind as to wait in the hall? I promise it won't be long. And shut the door. I know all about vampires and their hearing."

My eyes widen and meet Leonidas's. He shrugs in confusion. "I will. It was very nice meeting you, Ms. Manoie. Thank you... for the information."

I stand and walk out of the room, closing the door gently behind me. I can hear the murmur of voices still, so I walk a little way down the hall to give them some privacy. A few minutes later, Leonidas emerges, wiping away the last vestiges of the blood tears he shed due to whatever his mom said. I don't ask, but I slip my arm through his and walk with him through the maze of hallways. I don't say anything and neither does he as we reach the truck. He opens the passenger door for me and I climb in. He starts to close it and stops. Looking at the building, he says, "Thank you. I'm glad you came with me tonight." He quickly shuts the door and moves around the truck to get in.

He starts the truck and turns on the radio. He obviously needs a minute, and I don't mind. I could use my own minute. What the hell was his mom talking about? What do I need to make a choice about? Is it the guys? Maybe she told Leonidas a little more. How did she know we are vampires? Did he tell his mom that he was and she just assumed I would be too? Lady, you left me with a lot more questions, and I don't know if I want to pursue the answers. Her warning rings in my ears again, "It will be another thousand years of darkness if you fail." Sounds a lot like I don't have a choice in the matter. Fucking mystics and their lack of answers. Here is the question you need. Fuck off about the answer. You get to figure that out all by your lonesome because fuck you. I wonder if I could get to see her during the day? Maybe she would tell me more if I go by there without Leonidas. I need to get my car back from Mikael's place, anyway. I can pick it up tomorrow and visit her. If that is even possible. If it will even do any good. What moron would put the fate of the world on my shoulders? I have done a bang-up job of fucking up my life. Now some asshole in charge wants me to fuck up the rest of the planet? For the next thousand years. No pressure at all...

I look over at Leonidas. He still seems lost in thought as he drives us to wherever we are going. Some guys can look tough when they try to and others look tough just as part of who they are, but Leonidas looks dangerous. Tough was probably him as a teen. I don't know what his life has been like, but I would not bet against him having killed more than a few people before he became a vampire. Considering how I met him, I can only guess that his body count went up astronomically. How does a guy that would casually take his gang and kill an entire trailer park full of people also keep his 100-year-old mom in a fancy nursing home, visiting her every Monday night? He could have killed her at any time. And it sounds like she had a lot of her own problems and wasn't able to be the mom she felt she needed to be. But here he is, devoted as hell. He held a glass of water for her while she spoke, waiting for her to need it again. This, from the guy that exudes danger from his pores. The guy that called me little bunny and slapped me with the ultimatum of join us or die the first night I saw him.

* * *

We turn off into a parking lot and I decide that for tonight; I am going to do my best to let it go. This is the first actual date I have been on in years. I want to enjoy whatever he has planned as much as I can.

I can tell there is a building here and other cars, but it is really quiet and no lights. I shoot him a questioning look, but he just grins and shuts off the truck. "Come on, let's go see if you like this surprise better." He gets out and meets me at the front of the truck. He slips my arm through his and leads the way. Opening the door, a long hallway with dark blue carpet just thick enough to muffle the sound of steps, greets us. We follow the hallway around a curve to find a man sitting on a stool outside a door. He appears to have been waiting for us and stands as we approach.

"Hello Mr. Knight, your seats are just inside the door. We ask that you be as quiet as possible seating yourselves. The presentation has already begun." Leonidas nods and the man flips a switch on the wall, throwing the hall into darkness before he opens the door. I can hear a man speaking as we seat ourselves in the two open chairs next to the door. I tune in to the speaker and he is talking about stars and planets. Leonidas taps my arm and points up. I look up and the ceiling is open over me, stars glittering in their spaces as the man up front speaks. There is a screen behind him that shows blown up pictures of whatever he is speaking on at the moment. It looks like he is taking us through the planets currently. Saturn is on the screen and it is slowly zooming into the rings. I have never been to an observatory for any reason, much less for a date. My dates usually took me to a secluded spot where we could get busy. My heart is exploding with joy as I listen to the lecture on Saturn's rings. I look at Leonidas and find him watching me. I don't want to disturb anyone by speaking, so I throw my arms around him and hug him tight. His arms slip around me and he squeezes back. I release him and he leaves his arm on the back of the seat. Smooth sir, very smooth. But I find his arm feels nice on the chair behind me, the hand resting on my arm comforting. I lean over toward him and snuggle into his shoulder as I watch the presentation.

Two hours later, we exit through the same door and head for his truck. He opens the door for me to climb in before going around to get in the driver's seat. He starts the truck, saying, "I wasn't sure you would like that, so I had a back-up plan. Would you like to extend the evening, or do you need to get home?"

"I think I would like to extend the evening. I don't really know you and the observatory isn't good for talking. But can we do something quiet? The noise of the club is a lot most nights, so anything quiet is amazing in my world."

He grins, saying, "I didn't expect that. But I know a place." He puts the truck in drive and off we go.

The things his mom said are still swimming in my head as he drives. I need to either talk to him about them or about something else. I choose to bite the bullet in general and get the hard things over with, so I ask him, "Has your mom ever done anything like that before?"

He frowns, saying, "Not quite like that, no. There have been times when she told me not to go somewhere, something bad would happen. Times when she insisted we travel a different route. But no, nothing quite like that. I would like to say it is her age, she is a hundred years old, but I don't think it is. It is pretty certain that you should heed her warnings. I will make changes in my gang very soon. For one, start calling it a clan instead of a gang. Titles mean something, and clan implies family. I am going to turn them into something else. My mom, even if this is new, she is never wrong. When she would insist that we had to go another route, we would get where we were going and find out that there had been a massive accident on the route we had planned to take."

My heart sinks and I say, "So she is probably spot on with this stuff, too?"

He grimaces, telling me, "I'm afraid she likely is. I mean, there is a slight chance she could be off. But I wouldn't bet against her. I actually have a question for you about what she said. What did she mean when she said you took nearly all his power?"

Well, fuck. Now I've done it. Taking a breath I answer him, "I am going to tell you something that I really need you to keep secret. People would probably want me dead, people that could make me dead and ashes, that is. I need you to promise me you will keep what I say to you tonight between us."

He presses his lips together, then says, "I promise. I thought it might be like that, considering what she said about secrets."

"Exactly. This one has to be kept, or I am likely to be dead soon. Mikael had powers because of some things he did in his past. His actions aren't my story to tell, so I can't share that, but the long and short of it is that he ended up with special abilities and powers. Well, he refused to change anyone after that, because of his concern that he would pass on what he considered a curse. He wasn't wrong. When I goaded him into changing me he passed on, apparently most of the powers he had gained. I don't have to stay out of the sunlight. It has no effect on me. More importantly, he had magic. I don't know how to use it, but it looks like I took the lion's share of it."

His face in the light from the dash is shocked, his mouth open and eyes wide as he turns into what looks like a bookstore parking lot. He parks the truck and turns it off before turning in his seat to look at me. "You can walk in the day?"

I lift one shoulder in a shrug, saying, "Theoretically, yes. But I usually don't because I worry about others finding out and I don't know if that can be taken from me or even just shared with others. But I worry other vampires would not appreciate it. Plus, Mikael offered to kill me if I let it slip to anyone, so there's that."

"Wait, what? He offered to kill you?"

"All that and you stick on him offering to kill me? I mean, he isn't even the first guy to offer to kill me."

He blinks at me, mouth open like he has things to say. He shakes his head and says, "We are going to circle back to that. I got stuck on it because he is trying to date you, but at the same time is willing to kill you if you let a secret slip. But we can come back to that. You are probably correct in thinking that other vampires would want to kill you or take it from you, the ability to walk in the sunlight. I don't know if you are concerned about it, but considering what my mom said, I think it is very unlikely that it or the powers you have now can be taken from you. Whether any of it can be shared with someone else, well, that is questionable. I think the only reason that any of it was passed on to you was due to it waiting for you. Mikael was the vessel, so to speak."

"He will not like that. He believes women with magic will only do evil."

"What? Jeez-fuck-shit-dumbass. Don't tell me more about what he thinks for a little while. He is much older than I am and vampires get stronger with age. If I take him on, it will be with a plan or when I have no other choice.

Let's go in. I think you will love this and we could both use the distraction."

We get out of the truck and head toward the building. "Is this a bookstore? It looks like a bookstore."

"It is a bookstore. The only one I know of that is open twenty-four hours a day, seven days a week. They have a massive selection and they don't get mad if they find someone sleeping in the stacks. They just wake them up and bring them a complimentary cup of coffee. Apparently it happens pretty frequently, but the people that fall asleep here generally buy more books, so the owner decided it was good business sense to go with it."

He opens the door, and I am greeted by an enormous building full of books on shelves and on tables, just books everywhere. It looks so much bigger on the inside that I wonder if maybe the owner isn't a witch of some sort. My heart swells as I wander through the shelves and tables. So much knowledge just lying around here.

I remember I came here with someone and lift my head to look around for Leonidas. He is right behind me, a small smile on his face. "I think that is the softest I have ever seen your face."

H seems puzzled so I explain, "Most of the time you exude this aura of danger. You look like murder waiting to happen. All hard planes and angles, no give anywhere. Right now, you look sweet. It's nice on you."

He shoves his hands in his pockets, saying, "I was watching you be enchanted by the books. It made me smile. Don't tell people. You'll ruin my reputation and I'll have to kill people to fix it."

I laugh, "Sure thing, but I think your cover will be

blown anyway if any of your people find out how much thought you put into this date." We wander through the bookstore and I try not to pick anything up, until I remember I can.

"Dammit. When does this end? When do I not need to remember that I can take home books without the worry that my stupid husband will destroy them?"

Leonidas puts an arm around my shoulders, "Are there books we need to go back and pick up before we continue to explore the store?" he asks as he gives me a little squeeze.

I shake my head no, "No, if there is anything I want that bad, we can stop back by for it after we finish. I just, I feel like I should be over this already. Fabio is dead, I saw the body or well, what was left of it. I shouldn't still be reacting to the way he was. He isn't my problem anymore."

Leonidas nods, "You know, my mother is a hundred years old. She had me young because of traumatic incidents. You saw her tonight. She's still affected by them. I have my own past that affects me in ways I don't want to talk about. It isn't fair to expect to be healed and over everything in a week, month, sometimes even in years."

Sigh, "You may have a point. It would be a lot cooler if you didn't."

After wandering the store for a while longer, I have collected several books and we head for the checkout. The woman standing behind the counter is taking care of another customer as we walk toward her, but she stops speaking and turns her head to stare at us. I feel something like an icy breeze move over us and then she turns back to the other customer like nothing happened. We wait while she finishes with them and she watches the person leave before looking at us, saying, "You are a strange pair, aren't you? Tell me, how did you get the powers?"

My jaw falls open. "How did you know?"

She offers a tight smile, saying, "I have powers of my own. Answer the question or get out."

"Wow, that's rude. I got them when I was turned. The guy that turned me had them and I ended up with a lot of them. He got them a very long time ago. Wait, are you worried that I would try for your power?" Her mouth lifts in a half smile as I ramble, "I wouldn't do that. There are a lot of things I can be okay with, but I am not trying to steal anyone's power. These were just a bonus to being a vampire."

By the end of my little speech Leonidas is grinning at me and the lady behind the counter is shaking her head, "I would ask more, but if you are like any other vampire I have met you won't tell someone else's story. So, have you had any training?"

"There are people that will train you?"

She lifts a hand and rubs her temples, saying, "Yes. Because nobody wants a powerful witch running around with no training. What the hell, I may as well because my deities are surely not going to let me walk away from this. Would you like to be my student?"

I look at Leonidas, he shrugs and I look back at her, saying, "Maybe? I mean, I don't even know your name. Why would you do this for me?"

She sighs and looks up at the ceiling, asking, "Why? Am I living too quietly? I don't need the excitement, I can assure you. We are having such a talk when I get home." She looks back at me, introducing herself, "My name is Helen

Bastelle. I wouldn't do this for you personally just after meeting you. But I would do this because you are leaking magic all over my store and who knows what kind of havoc you are going to wreak if you don't learn to control your powers. I am doing it for my lovely little city, so it will stay in one piece. So that all the races that aren't supposed to exist aren't revealed in one fell swoop by an accidental spell or explosion of accidental magic. It isn't really for you specifically. The fact that you benefit is no more than a side effect."

I chuckle, "When you put it that way, it sounds so much more enticing. I accept. However, I am on a date right now so maybe we could meet tomorrow or something? Maybe I could give you my number? Ooh, wait. No. Not my number. That phone came from Mikael. I have to get a new one. Sorry, no one calls me, so I just forgot."

Leonidas crosses his arms in front of him, "He took away your phone and provided you with a new one?"

"Yes. Yes. I know. Look, I'll get another one on the way to work tomorrow. Give me a break. I've been a little busy." I roll my eyes at him and turn back to Helen, saying, "Can I meet you somewhere or something?"

She chuckles, "Maybe my deities decided I need entertainment. Yes, you can meet me here Wednesday night, and we can talk more then. For now, let's do something about the magic you are leaking all over the place." She walks around the counter and holds her hands up, palms facing me. When she looks expectantly at me and I put my hands up in front of hers, just a little away from hers. She lifts a brow at me, saying, "You'll need to trust me eventually. For tonight, this will do." She moves her hands forward till they are flush with mine. She whispers some words. They are strange to my ears and seem almost slippery. When she stops, I feel dizzy for just a split second and then I feel like a hole is stoppered? Like I had been being drained and now the leak was patched.

"Holy shit, you were serious. Is it going to hurt me to have all this bottled up in me?"

"No. You were meant to have this magic in you. You may not have gotten it in the usual way, but it is definitely yours. Anything that wasn't would have left you for the original owner when I did the first part of that spell."

"Looks like I'm not the only one with trust issues."

She lifts a shoulder, saying, "You aren't wrong. Now, let's get you checked out. I feel another customer almost done shopping."

She rings up my purchases and Leonidas pays before I can, his grin of delight making me laugh. Helen looks at me as she grabs another book from under the counter and places it in my bag. "Start reading this. It will help you get a grip on things." She slides the bag over as the other customer appears out of the shelves. I nod and, lifting the bag, we leave.

* * *

Leonidas takes me back home after the bookstore. We talk about the weirdness of the evening on the way home. He tells me that he has never had a first date quite this exciting and I tell him I have never had one so nice. He grunts and clears his throat, saying, "I'm glad you enjoyed the evening."

He pulls into my driveway and puts the truck in park. I look over at him, asking, "Would you like to come in?"

He slants a look at me, saying, "I very much would. It is getting close to sunrise, though. Are you certain you want me here that long?"

I grin, telling him, "Well, I was going to use that as an excuse to keep you here for longer."

He laughs, saying, "Cat's out of the bag now." He shuts off the truck and we get out.

In the trailer he says, "Why haven't you put any furniture in here?"

"I don't know. I... maybe I just don't know what I want in here? Would you like a drink? I have scotch, vodka, or blood. Heh, I could make you a bloody Mary."

He shakes his head at me, saying, "I'll take a scotch."

I make our drinks, handing his over I say, "Come on, the bed is the most comfortable place to be. I knew what I wanted for that." But as I turn to lead the way and then I stop in my tracks, "You can't, um, you can't make fun of me for this." I turn to look at him.

His brows pulled down and a frown on his lips, he asks, "Make fun of what? Why would I make fun of you for anything?"

I look at the carpet, old and ratty but still easier to deal with than this, saying, "My bed. You can't make fun of my bed. It's frilly and girly, and if you make fun of it, you're getting a throat punch."

He is silent. I look up from the carpet to see him looking angry. As fearsome as he looks, I have no fear of him. I know he will never lay a hand on me to hurt, now. My only concern is that instead of the happy ending I planned for tonight, I will be arguing with him when he says, "Who?"

I tip my head to one side, saying, "I don't understand?"

He tosses back the scotch, "Who teased you and taunted you about everything to the point that you would feel the need to tell someone not to make fun of your bed?"

Clarity dawns and I realize he isn't mad at me. He is mad at the person who did this. My jaw drops and my eyes go round as I ask, "You aren't mad at me, are you?"

He shakes his head no slowly, growling, "I am not. Yet."

"It was my husband. You saw where I lived. There was none of me in it. Because every part of me that I shared he made fun of. It was always just a joke. I was too sensitive. But it never felt like jokes to me, so I just got rid of it all." I gulp down my drink and extend my hand for his glass, asking, "Would you like another? Or maybe the bottle?"

He hands me his glass with a curt nod. I slip past him and refill our glasses. Returning to stand in front of him, I hold his glass out to him. He looks hard at me for a long moment. Finally, he takes the glass and says, "The husband is the one my people killed?"

"He was. The only husband I had in this life. At this point, he is likely to become the only one I have ever had in this life. Would you like to see my bed now?"

"I would. Thank you." He follows behind me and my nerves are pinging. Please, oh please, don't let him hate it. I step into the room and off to the side. He is the first to see it now that I have finished it. I squeezed a king size bed in the room. The delivery guys didn't want to leave it here with little ol' me. They were worried I couldn't get it in... I covered it in pillows and ruffles, all of it pink, white, and glitter with a sleigh frame and white tulle hung from the ceiling to drift down on each corner of the bed.

He stops in the doorway, studying the bed. He finally says, "That's a lot of ruffles. Is it comfortable?"

"Surprisingly, yes. Also, it is great fun to sweep all the pillows off and onto the floor. I am entertained every time I do it. So far, I don't even mind picking them up the next evening."

He grins, "Can I try it?"

I take a sip of my drink, saying, "You want to shove my pillows off the bed? Sure, why not? Go for it."

He passes his drink to me and, standing at the foot of the bed, he leans over and sweeps pillows from the side nearest me across the bed and off onto the floor. Most of them also hit the wall but as they are pillows, the velocity did no injury to the wall.

He straightens with a grin, saying, "That was oddly satisfying."

I hand him his drink and climb on the bed as I say, "It really is. Come, sit up here among the ruffles." Keeping my feet hanging off the bed, I unzip my boots and kick them off. He toes off his boots and climbs on the bed. I lay on my side and he follows suit, facing toward me.

He looks completely at ease among the ruffles and pink as he sips his scotch. All traces of the anger from earlier are gone like they never existed. I swirl my drink in my glass, telling him, "Tonight was... a lot."

He nods, "It was. Definitely an unforgettable first date."

I laugh, "It is that. What do you think your mom meant when she said I would change the world?"

"If I understand her right, something you do will change things. The question is whether or not those things will be beneficial. Based on what she said, it looks like the good or ill depends on who you choose to be with. I guess the company you keep really is that important."

"Did she give you any clues about who would help me change things for the better?"

He grins at me, saying, "She said you would ask that and that there was no right answer for me to give. So, for once, I am just going to take her advice and keep things to myself."

"That is supremely helpful." I smile to let him know I am not at all irritated. His mom is right. There is no right answer for him to give there, so it is better that he doesn't answer the question. Even if it is frustrating that I can't just be given the answer. "Do you think Helen really meant what she said? About helping me because it benefits her? And everyone else? That it would really be that dangerous for me to be walking around leaking magic?"

He finishes his scotch before answering, "I don't know anything about magic. For that matter, until I was bitten, I didn't know anything about anything. I know she wasn't lying. Whether what she says is true, it is what she believes. I will say that she knew you had magic in you. If I had to guess, I would say she knew someone was in there with a lot of magic and was having trouble pinpointing who it was until we got close to her. That, coupled with her reluctance to take you on as a student, suggests that she is probably accurate in her statements. Are you concerned about meeting with her for lessons?"

"A little." I finish the last bit of my scotch, "What if's keep running through my head and... I am pretty afraid of dying."

He lifts a brow, saying, "I'm sorry, what?"

"I know it's silly. But I was trying to leave my husband. Again. He didn't want me, but wouldn't let me go either. When you and your gang killed him, you set me free, accident that it was. That is why I was willing to do anything to stay free. Who knew I would find another vampire lurking under my trailer as I ran from you? I thought for sure you would just kill me no matter what you said. Now, now I'm seeing a couple of guys. I work as a dancer and I'm a vampire with a bonus. As fucked up as things have been in the past few weeks, my life is grand as compared to what I had before. The idea of dying right now... Just as my life is getting good. It terrifies me. There isn't much I wouldn't do to keep living. Heh, that's why I had no problems killing your guys. I would apologize, but I am not sorry."

He laughs, saying, "I wouldn't expect an apology for that. I would have done the same and I may be a lot of things, but a hypocrite is one I try to avoid." He plucks my glass from my hands and sets both glasses on the floor next to the bed. As he turns to face me again, I crawl across the bed to settle on top of him and he quickly positions himself to be laying on his back. Smiling up at me, he says, "Done talking?"

I set my hands on his belly, smiling when he sucks air in a hiss. As I run my hands up to his top button, I say, "Do you know why I stopped to listen to you when you spoke that first night?"

His hands find my thighs and grip them lightly as I start with the buttons on his shirt, "No, I don't."

"Your voice. Your voice is sexy as sin on a dark night. Every time you speak, I want to do some of the most sinful things to you," I reach the end of his buttons, "but before I go further, are you good with doing these sinful things that feel so very good? No is an acceptable answer too. We can just continue drinking and talking."

I wait with my hands still on his shirt. He smiles slow and sexy, "Babe, I think I might die tonight if you don't finish what you are starting here." He rocks his hips with excruciating slowness and as his hardness presses into me, I let my head fall back. Straightening, I snatch his shirt the rest of the way open and out of his pants. His hands caress my thighs as I lightly run my nails up his belly, flattening my hands to appreciate his sculpted chest. I take my hands from his body, saying, "One moment. Don't move."

He groans as I move off him to remove my pants, saying, "I didn't want to be too presumptuous by snatching these off before you consented." Pants out of the way, I hop back on top of him and watch as his eyes go directly to my panties. I grin and grab the bottom edge of my shirt, revealing an inch of skin at a time. His eyes are glued to the bottom edge of my shirt and his hands have returned to my thighs, his thumbs teasing at the edge of my panties. I press down a little as I lift my shirt off and toss it.

His moan excites me and I use my feet to press his legs together, lifting myself and scooting back a little as I work on opening his jeans. His cock rises as I unzip him. I grin at him and lean down to give the tip a lick before I work his pants off. With those safely deposited on my floor, I crawl back up to take him in my mouth. He winds his fingers in my hair and is quickly tugging me upward, groaning, "That isn't how I want to go tonight. Maybe some other time. For now..." He wraps his arms around me and rolls us over, coming to rest between my legs, he presses his length against me.

I moan, "Leonidas," and he leans back.

Looking down at my panties, he asks, "Are you very attached to these?"

I shake my head no and he grabs the sides, snatching the fabric apart on one side and then the other. He pulls the fabric away and tosses it. Grabbing my legs, he lifts me up as he leans in to give my pussy a long swipe with his tongue, murmuring, "Gods, you taste good." Another lick has my nerve endings humming. He eases me down to the bed, my legs fall open before him as he moves forward. He twines his fingers in my hair as his tip touches my wet entrance.

He brings his lips to mine, kissing me hard as his cock drives into me. I moan in my throat as he fucks me hard and fast. I rock my hips just so with my legs spread wide, and he is hitting my clit just right. Screaming as I cum hard on his cock. He slows his thrusts and grins, growling, "Like that, do you? Wait till you see my next trick."

He pulls out and flips me over onto my hands and knees. I feel him guide himself back into me, and I close my eyes to savor the stretching sensation. He buries himself completely in me and leans forward over me. One hand on my belly sliding down to rub my clit as he pinions his hips behind me. His other hand wraps in my hair and he pulls me up with him, his cock never breaking its rhythm. He nibbles my ear and moves down my neck, nipping.

I moan, "Oh god, Leonidas, bite me."

His thrusts pick up speed and the fingers rubbing my clit press just a little harder. I moan and he sinks his fangs into my neck. I scream with the orgasm that rushes through my body, every nerve ending on fire with the pleasure of it all as he thrusts hard into me one more time, his own orgasm spilling from him. He releases my neck and we both fall to lie spent on the bed.

Reality rushes in as I realize I told him to bite me and I don't know what my blood will do to him. My eyes widen. What if Mikael finds out? "Oh shit, Leonidas. I may have fucked up."

MIKAEL

I'M WALKING through the city and the sky looks strange. It seems red, but it isn't sunrise or sunset. I don't recognize the area I am walking through. The buildings are tall and nondescript. People are walking past and they don't seem to see me. I come to a break in the buildings. Turning my head, I see Jasmine standing in the middle of a stream. I walk toward her and the world changes around me. Before me, Jasmine stands in the stream still. On the far side of the stream, I see a meadow and, in the distance, a small town. Behind me is a shining city bustling with activity. The sidewalk I am on stops at the stream. To either side of the sidewalk, the land is blasted. A wasteland of death on this side of the stream, except for the shining city behind me.

I walk the rest of the way to Jasmine. Why is she standing in the stream? As I reach her and she lifts her head to smile radiantly at me. I reach out to caress her face and she places her palm flush with mine before I can. Mildly annoying, but I'll let it slide. I look up from our hands and she turns her smile on Leonidas, who has appeared on the other side of the stream.

He puts his hand up, and she places her palm flush to his. I try to move my hand to pull her to me, but I can't move. Jasmine turns her face to the sky and screams in pain, tears flowing down her face. I try to move, my muscles don't respond. I growl in frustration. My eyes meet Leonidas's and he smirks at me.

Jasmine's scream fades, and she turns tear-filled eyes to me. She says, "Goodbye Mikael."

Her hand leaves mine, and she steps to Leonidas. He pulls her into his arms. His smug face turns to watch me. I can finally move and then I am falling, the ground beneath me gone as I watch them disappear. I hit the ground hard and I jump up. What is this place? It looks like ruins of some sort. How did I get here? Turning a slow circle, taking in the details, verdant greenery everywhere, once stately and modern buildings falling to pieces. I see a sidewalk leading out of this place into a huge grassy meadow. Following the sidewalk to its end outside the city where it stops at a small stream, just like the one Jasmine stood in... I look up and in the distance I see a small town.

My eyes fly open as I sit straight up in the bed. My bedding is destroyed from my thrashing, blanket and sheet somehow on either side of the bed. I realize I am breathing hard, as if I had run for miles. I focus on my breathing, slowing it and calming myself.

That dream was so real. And Jasmine appeared to me as she is now, not as she was when we were wed. A shame, I really liked that form. But this dream. It felt too real. I know the wizard could occasionally see into the future. Is the power I stole from him trying to warn me of impending trouble?

Is Jasmine really thinking about being with that gang banger Leonidas Knight? I think back over the dream, after she crossed the stream to him, was when the dream went to hell... That's it! It's warning me that my life will never be the same if I let her go now. I have to woo her. She can't be allowed to choose him over me. She would be a fool to choose him, anyway. Helping her see that should be cake and I love cake.

** * **

Much later, I pull up to Jasmine's trailer. I put the window down and while I smell the remnants of the party had by the trailer up front recently, I can tell Jasmine isn't here. If I want to talk to her tonight, I'll have to go to the club. Club Amnesia. I hate that she works there. The place is awful and the people there are trash. I can't tell her that, I think as I look around the place she chooses to live in. Backing out of her driveway, I point the car toward the club. I don't know if I can bring myself to wait inside. I think I'll just wait near the back. If I park down the street, no one will notice me or bother me. It is only a couple hours till she gets done there. The only benefit I see to that place is the ready access to blood she has from patrons requesting private sessions.

I wonder if she pays off the owner to not watch when she gives a private session? Or maybe the bouncer? I know they aren't supposed to touch the girls, but maybe this place is less rule following than I imagine?

I pull into a lot down the street from the club. It is

mostly deserted, but I park in a less well lit corner away from the building. Checking the time, I see it is nearly two. I won't have to wait as long as I thought I would. She should get off work any time now. Getting out of the car, I check the air, but I don't smell Leonidas or any of his gang bangers in the vicinity. My hands in my pockets, I stroll toward the club. I get to the last lamp post before the back door and I lean against it to wait. Jasmine always comes out this way and seeing me will comfort her, knowing she doesn't need to concern herself with anyone attacking her.

I have only waited ten minutes or so when the back door opens and Jasmine steps out. I smile at her though her attire, sexy as it is, makes me cringe that she would wear it in public. The cutoff shorts with fishnet stockings and heeled combat boots are bad enough, but pairing it with a distressed tank top and that ratty backpack we took from the kid on her first night as a vampire is just too much.

I step away from the light pole as she walks toward me, her hands clutching the straps of her backpack, probably ashamed to have me see her like this. I want her to be at ease so I step forward as she draws near and spread my arms for a hug, "Jasmine, I've missed you."

She smiles a small smile and hugs me. Wrapping my arms around her feels so good, so right. I love having her here, now if I can just convince her to stay here. Better yet to move back to the house. I release her and she steps back. "Mind if I walk you home? Or we can drive if you prefer."

She studies my face for long minutes. I wish I knew what she was thinking. She nods and says, "You can walk me home. I enjoy the night air."

I step to the side and thread my arm through hers as we walk toward her place. "So how was work?"

She tenses, "It was good. I made a thousand dollars tonight even though it was kind of slow."

I lift a brow, saying, "Kind of slow? The parking lot looked full."

She shrugs and takes her arm out of mine. "Yeah, that is kind of slow. We usually have them parked all around the block. Tonight, it looks like they pretty well fit in the parking lot."

I nod and slip my hands into my pocket with a frown. "You seem stand-offish tonight, everything ok?"

She sighs, "I'm fine. But I never want to be touched right after I get off work. I spend my time in there dancing and letting strangers drool over me. By the end of the night, I need some space for just me."

"I see. You know, you could always come live at the house. You wouldn't have to work and you could take whatever you have saved up to invest. It might be good for you to relax for a few years. Let me take care of you. Here," I stop and pull out the bank card I have carried in my wallet for some time now, "I created an account for you. Use it as you will. I have it set up so that money is wired to it monthly. There is plenty in there to take care of you so that you don't have to work."

Holding the card out to her, I watch as she shakes her head no, saying, "I can't take your money. I don't want you giving me money thinking that will buy me. That isn't how this works, Mikael."

I take her hand and press the card into it, "I promise, this money is yours. When we wed, I was given a sizable estate to hold in trust for you. I can promise you that the money going into that account is from that original estate. I kept it for you because you always hated asking me for money. But the laws in that time forbade you from having full control of your own money. So take the money. I will finish transferring all of that into the account and then sever the connection with my accounts. Ok?"

She studies my face. Sighing, she nods, "Ok. If you swear this money is from an estate you had solely because of me and you will sever the payment set up once it is all trans-ferred in, fine."

I release her hand, leaving the card. She slips it into a pocket. Pulling out the envelope with the pin number in it, I hand that over as well. It goes in another pocket. We walk again and I ask, "How did your date with Leonidas go?"

I hope for a report of dullness and her refusal to see him again, but she smiles, "It went well. I don't think you really want to hear about that, though. Anything exciting happening at the house? How are Chloe and Scarlett?"

I shrug, "They are well. I think they miss having you there. Morhall is quiet and peaceful. Possibly a little boring without you there. I miss your presence in the house."

"I'm not coming back, Mikael. I need to be on my own, to live as I please without the interference of anyone. You know I spent too long, too many lifetimes trapped in marriages that kept me from being me. I will not be tied to any one person now."

"I suppose I do understand that. I feel relieved, to be honest, that you aren't rushing into anything with Leonidas. He is not a good person."

"Why? Because he murders people? We do the same

thing. I murdered someone the first night after I became a vampire. And more since then. I can assure you, that is not weighing on my conscience even a little. I almost feel like I could thank him for killing my husband and setting me free."

Frowning, I look over at her. She has a smile on her face when she talks about him. I don't like it. I need to change her opinion of him. Maybe I can tie the guy she killed that first night to Leonidas somehow. She hated him for involving kids. It bears looking into. "I was thinking, we haven't been out on a date in centuries. May I take you out one night this week?"

Her face scrunches in concentration. She is adorable. She looks up at me, saying, "I have Sunday night off. Would that work for you?"

"You don't have Wednesday off this week?" I ask, narrowing my eyes.

She raises a brow at me, saying, "I traded with a girl that wanted Wednesday off. What's with the suspicion Mikael? Shouldn't you just be pleased that I will go out with you at all?"

Ooops. Well, that backfired. "Of course I am! I am disappointed that I won't get to take you out sooner than Sunday night. I understand, of course, duty calls. I would like to point out that you could just leave the job."

She rolls her eyes at me, the brat! "Mikael, I like my job. I like the girls I work with. I enjoy doing something society deems inappropriate. Honestly, I am wondering about tattoos right now. Do they stick now that I am immortal?"

I shrug, telling her, "For a few years. Ten, maybe. After that, they are so faded as to be non-existent or just completely gone. Sunday night? That gives me time to plan something really grand. I'll send something fancy over for you. I want you to feel like the princess you are. You are going to have a great time."

She laughs, saying, "You're like a kid let loose in a candy store. I'm looking forward to it. I haven't felt like a princess in... Ever. It'll be nice to feel like a princess, even if it is only for a night."

Seventeen

JASMINE

I ARRIVE at the bookstore early for my meeting with Helen. As I wander around the shelves, I am immersed in the titles available. I am so distracted that when Helen steps into the aisle and calls my name; it startles me and I jump. She chuckles, "I understand. Books make me happy too. Come, let's go to the back."

I follow her as she winds her way through shelves and tables through a door marked Employees Only. It looks very official, but I don't pause as I follow her through. The back area is vast. There are boxes everywhere in various stages of unpack. She leads me past those and down a hall to the right. The third door we come to, she opens and walks in. I ask if she wants the door open or closed and she says, "Close it. That activates the spell to keep any wayward magic within these walls."

Curious, I watch closely as I close the door to see if I can tell. I see a faint ripple around the edges, but nothing more. Helen is watching me from where she sits at a table across the room. As I walk over, she asks, "What did you see?"

I tell her about the ripple and she nods, "Good. Good. Come sit. Did you read any of the book?"

"I did. I was mostly confused by it. Why do I need to still my mind? And it said nothing about how to access my magic at all."

"We start slow with the accessing magic. Though I have a feeling you will need to go faster than most." She sniffs at the air around me. "You smell like a whole lot of trouble coming your way." When I look confused, she says, "As you become more adept with the magic, you will develop your own ways of intuiting things. For me, it is smells. Some people see auras or visions. Others hear things on the wind. What matters now is that you learn how to access your magic. We will start small, but as you have an awful lot of magic in you, I am going to enclose you in a bubble. You will be able to walk out of it, but it will keep things from spreading. Now, I need you to center yourself. However that looks, if it is deep breathing or chants or whatever. Once you feel centered, I want you to light this candle." She flicks her fingers and I see a transparent bubble appear around me. Then she pushes a tea light candle into the space.

I close my eyes and just try to collect myself. To let go of the nerves eating at me as I wait to find out whether Leonidas has gained anything from drinking my blood. The worry about what Mikael will do if he finds out I let anyone, let alone Leonidas, drink my blood. But mercy, it felt so damn good. I shake my head, focus Jasmine. Two slow deep breaths as I reach for the core of me. It's strange, but I feel like I found the power inside myself. Opening my eyes and focusing on lighting the candle. Imagining a flame on the wick in my mind so I just work on making that picture as strong as I can. I hear a little pop and I see the entire candle is on fire. I frown, "A little too much."

Helen grins and near shouts, "Excellent work! Few even get a flame on their first try. You set the whole candle on fire! Oh, you are going to be so fun when you get trained!" She grabs an empty glass and flips it over, putting the brim on the table so the candle is enclosed within the cup. The flames quickly die leaving the cup smoke-filled and sooty.

"I did well? Even though I set the whole candle on fire?"

"Yes, you did. You did magic on your first try and that is sort of amazing. It happens but rarely enough that it thrills me when I get to see it."

We spend the next few hours with me practicing doing various minor tasks. By the time we quit for the night, I can reliably light candles, call a breeze, shield myself, and shield someone else. Though my shielding of someone else needs work.

I trapped Helen inside a shield while practicing. She couldn't leave it and I couldn't get in. She was just so amazing the whole time. Never got mad and was so patient while I figured it out. By the end, we were laughing and giggling like old friends. I had the best time with her. Now she is walking me out of the bookstore, telling me, "Most magic comes from a place of love and happiness. And that is a good thing. Sometimes there is no love or laughter to be had, only fear and anger. Whatever comes from those last two will be harsh and unforgiving. I know you are old enough to know this, but we cannot take some things back, and that is doubly true for magic. Your magic can't hurt you, but it can hurt the ones you love if you cast in anger. Keep that in mind."

I nod, "I will. I don't want to hurt anyone by accident."

Helen eyes me. "Don't think I didn't notice the distinction, and appreciate it. I know very well that some people won't allow you to be without a lesson that costs them dearly. Always be sure you intend what you do."

"I will. When do you want me to come by again?"

"Are Wednesday nights good for you? They are reliably a good time for me."

"I can make it work."

"Ok then. I will see you on Wednesday."

I wave goodbye as I step out into the night air.

Eighteen

JASMINE

I HAVEN'T SEEN Leonidas since our date, and I am a little concerned. He said he had to implement some changes within his gang, so possibly that is keeping him away. For now, it is just as well. I am getting dressed for my date with Mikael. He sent over a dress that is gorgeous. I feel bad taking it out of the package here. The top half is corseted, and it is fitted along the hips opening into an A shape with a split up one thigh. It is black with what I hope are rhinestones decorating the bust. The heels he sent match the dress, soft satiny black with stones encrusting the heels. My hair and makeup are done so I am just lounging on my bed till it is time to put the dress on. I don't want to mess it up or make it wrinkly lying around in it.

My phone chimes with the alarm I set. Time to put the dress on. I know Mikael will be punctual. I am just slipping on the shoes when I hear the car pull up. Moving carefully, I walk out of the trailer, the tiny purse he sent with the outfit in hand. Mikael is just getting out of the car and he stops, his mouth open for just a moment before he recovers. Hurrying over, he extends a hand to help me balance as I walk through the grass to the passenger seat. He opens the door with a flourish, saying, "Madame."

I giggle as I seat myself. Before he closes the door, he says, "You have identification with you, correct?"

Frowning, I reply, "I do, but why would I need it?"

He closes the door and, getting back into the driver's seat, he says, "That is part of the surprise."

I question him as he drives, but he won't give up any information. Then we arrive at the airport and he steers us through to the area with the private jets.

Swallowing, I try to breathe as we park. I've never flown anywhere. Ok, I can do this. I wait while he walks around to my door, letting him open it and give me his hand to assist me. We walk arm in arm into the building. The pilot comes to greet us, telling Mikael that he is just finishing up the paperwork and we are welcome to board. Mikael guides me to one of them and we climb the stairs to the jet. The inside is lovely, all cream-colored leather seats with gorgeous wood tables. Mikael leads me to a seat and after I seat myself, he sits across from me. A flight attendant brings us some wine fortified with blood, which I accept gratefully, as I tend to skip meals on nights I don't have to work.

The pilot comes through, letting us know that we will be taking off momentarily. Mikael nods and thanks the man as he heads for the cockpit. I sip the wine and try not to watch out the window as I hear the engines fire up.

"Talk to me Mikael. I've never flown before and I'm a little nervous. Do you fly often?"

He looks surprised but says, "I do. I have business in various places and sometimes a deal requires me to be there. You really have nothing to worry about. This will be a short trip. We aren't going that far. It is just much faster this way. We can drive home if you find you don't enjoy flying. Or even stay over and drive home tomorrow."

"Tell me about your life without me. What have you been doing all this time?"

He looks out the window, his lips pressed together, saying, "I spent a great deal of time watching you or searching for you. I have watched you grow old and pass away surrounded by a family that I despised for getting to be with you, but also loved because they seemed to make you happy. When I wasn't spending my time watching you or searching for where you were born this time, I worked at multiplying my assets. To some extent, I took care of that the entire time, as I was occasionally called away. Most times, I could content myself with simply being near you."

I shake my head, asking, "Why didn't you ever come out in the open, speak to me even once?"

He looks away from the view out the window, saying, "I always felt so guilty for being the reason you were killed. You barely got to live and then you were murdered so that he could get to me. If that weren't enough, then I went and got myself turned into a vampire. Damned for all eternity. The idea of bringing you into this, of damning your soul just so I could be part of your life... I felt like it would be the most selfish thing I had ever done." He downs the rest of his wine and holds the glass out. I watch as the flight attendant brings him a fresh glass, taking the old one away with her.

"Most of those other lives were more than a little awful in so many ways. I would have then, as I did in this time, welcomed any opportunity to be set free from the whole thing. I think perhaps you don't understand how hard life often is for women inside a marriage. Hell, fully half of those lives I was being beaten on the regular by my husband. I will say that feeling you out there sometimes comforted me. Even if it frustrated me and made me think I might be cracking up more than once."

"I did not know. Though if I had my choice, I wouldn't have turned you in this life either."

"Hmm, I feel like you got what you deserved there. You had no right to take my choice away like that, telling everyone that they could not turn me. I have no regrets, even now. My life is more than a little out of control, but it has never been better and I have the time to get it right. I thank you for turning me. Whatever may come, you have my gratitude for turning me."

He turns his gaze back out the window, asking, "Do you love me still?"

I smile softly. He keeps his gaze pointed to the window with his face so carefully neutral as I say, "I love you very much. Even after all this time, I still have a deep and abiding love in my soul for you."

He turns to me with a pained expression, "Then why won't you come home?"

I sip my drink, saying, "I can't. You don't understand that I am a whole person capable of making her own decisions. I don't know if you ever will. I know that I am in need of healing of the spiritual kind and that I need to do that living alone. Whatever may come, I am going to be in a better place before I will live with anyone. Way before I will commit to anyone."

He perks up at the last sentence, saying, "So you don't see yourself committing to anyone before you feel you are healed? Including Leonidas?"

Finishing my wine, I nod, "Correct. I am not willing to be in a full relationship unless I am in a good relationship with myself. My next relationship will be a healthy one or it won't be."

He smiles at that, saying, "I guess I need to take you out more often, so that we can get to know each other better. Do you enjoy dancing? Like ballroom dancing. Not referring to your job."

I think about it, "I don't know. I've never tried it."

"How do you feel about trying it?"

My eyes widen and I ask, "Is that what we are going to do tonight? Are we going dancing?" He nods and I squee a little, saying, "Are you going to teach me how to dance? I do not know how to. Is it a ball? Will everyone be dressed and ballroom dancing?"

He smiles, "Yes, it is a ball and yes, I will teach you to dance. Yes, everyone else will be dressed and will be ballroom dancing."

"Oooo, thank you! I can't wait! What kind of ball is it?"

"It is a fundraising ball for a museum. Very fancy, fit for a princess. They provided a dinner earlier but, well, we aren't going to do that justice. We will arrive in time for the entertainment and speeches, which will be followed by dancing. You will love it."

"What museum? Oh, who cares? Is it art or science or history or?"

"It is history. Having lived through a lot of it, I know firsthand how much is missing and I want to preserve what they can find and decide is factual."

"Fantastic. I can't wait. How much longer till we arrive?"

He checks his phone, saying, "Another ten minutes or so."

"Wonderful! Is the ball far from the terminal?" I ask as I set my glass in the holder on the table.

"It is about a twenty-minute drive, but we will have a driver and a fully stocked bar in the limo."

Fifteen minutes later, we are seated in the back of a limo speeding down the highway in a town I have never seen before now. I watch the buildings fly by as Mikael pours our drinks, vodka for him and scotch for me. He sits back and hands my drink over. His suit is really doing him all the justice tonight. He must have had it tailored, it fits him so well. Hugging his broad shoulders and tapering down to his hips. We arrive at the building the ball is being held in and are dropped off near the front door. Mikael gives an invitation to the man at the door while I notice we aren't the only ones who showed up after the food. Four other cars have pulled in as the doorman looked Mikael up on the list.

We are granted entry, and the inside is amazing. Everything sparkles, with glittering ribbons strung on waist high poles following the line of a red carpet to keep us going toward the main ballroom. Outside the ribbon barriers, they display various art pieces at intervals, as are the ever-present security.

We reach the doors and the men standing to either side open them before us. Mikael points to a two person table closer to the front, saying, "There is our table. The first speech should start soon." As we walk to our table, several people speak to Mikael and he introduces me to each of them. They are all very nice to me right now, in this place. We reach our seats and get seated just as the lights dim. The first speaker is the president of the museum, thanking everyone for their generous donations. She thanks each of her top donors personally by calling out their names and asking for a round of applause for them as the spotlight finds each of them. I watch the people stand as the spotlight finds them and they do a little bow before seating themselves again. Then she calls our names, sort of, when she says Mr. And Mrs. Mikael Harris. Mikael grabs my arm and we stand together. I smile and do the little bow as I grit out through my teeth in a low whisper, "What did she mean by Mr and Mrs?"

Mikael pretends not to hear me until the light swings elsewhere. "I thought it would be nice to show you off."

"I am fine with being shown off, but why didn't I get my own name?"

"Oh, that. I just think it sounds nicer this way. I love the old world way of announcing a married couple."

"We are not married Mikael. Don't do this again. If you decide to include me in something like this, you use my name. My name. I am my own person, not some extension of you."

"Yes, yes. I will. Look, the first act is coming out. They have a theatre company performing The Phantom of the Opera."

With one last glare at Mikael, I turn to see the curtains open for a much edited version of the opera. It is still amazing and the singers are wonderful. The intermission gives everyone the chance to walk around and mingle a bit. Mikael takes me around, introducing me to many more people, all of whom now think I am his wife. I laugh it off every time and make sure they know we are not actually married. Mikael seems less than pleased by this, especially as some of the single gentlemen eye me after that with a certain spark in their eyes.

We return to our seats once the bells chime. The performers finish the last half of the opera and it is so sad. I always feel like she should have gone with the phantom. I never understood why she went with the plain guy. All he had going for him was a title and a bank account. The phantom had the bank and all that sexy. He had issues, sure. But we all do. The curtains close on the last scene and I sigh.

Mikael turns to me, asking, "Are you unhappy?"

"No, I am not. The opera has a bittersweet ending, in my opinion. That's all the sigh was about."

He tips his head to one side, asking, "How would you have it end?"

I tell him my thoughts and I think I see his eyes narrow for just a heartbeat, but it is gone so fast I can't be certain. The music plays and he stands as he extends his hand to me, he says, "Care to dance my love?"

"I would like nothing better."

He leads me out to the dance floor among the other couples already dancing. He stops and turns, taking me in his arms. I follow his lead and the dance seems to flow, as if my feet remember the steps from another lifetime. We float through the dance floor for multiple songs. He tells me I look lovely and I dance even better. The band takes a break and we collect fresh drinks as we mingle.

Quite a few women give me dirty looks, but I'm not hating on them, they aren't really mad at me. I allow him to maneuver me into a darker corner, smiling up at him in expectation of some stolen kisses. He turns an angry visage to me and says, "Could you stop embarrassing me for the evening? Is there a reason you feel you must tell every single person who mentions my last name in connection to you we are not married? And why would you laugh? Is it really so laughable an idea that we could be married?"

My heart freezes in my chest. I thought we were having a great time. "Because I am Jasmine Felton, not Harris, and I will not pretend otherwise. Why did you set this up?"

He runs a hand through his hair, "I thought it would be nice, give you a chance to see what being with me would be like. How nice it could be to be Mrs. Harris. This is not going how I expected."

I rub my chest. The cold in there is nearly painful and I tell him, "I don't want to be married Mikael, not even to you. I appreciate this is what you want, but I need you to respect my wishes if this is to continue in any manner."

He nods, "I just, I really need you to pick me. I feel like..." he looks around the room and leans against the wall, "like this world is going to be destroyed if you choose him."

My eyes widen, and I quickly take a sip of my drink. Why would he say that? How would he know that? "Why," my voice cracks and I have to clear my throat, "why do you say that?"

He shrugs, saying, "I had this dream. It was weird, and I

woke up feeling like the world I know will be no more if you go down that path."

I look around at the glitz and the glamour of this place and I think about my life up to now. The trailer parks, the shit places I lived with my aunt before I could escape. All the neighborhoods I walk through sometimes when I need to think. The people that take advantage of the poor and could well be at a ball like this or this very one right now.

Looking over at Mikael, I say, "Maybe that wouldn't be such a bad thing."

Nineteen

CHLOE

I PUT on some long wear lip stain as the last of my preparations before I meet Scarlett and we head out for the night. We decided to visit one of the local clubs for our meal tonight, because bagged is great for the convenience but fresh and hot tastes so much better. Leaving my bedroom I can hear faint mutterings from downstairs. It sounds like Mikael but whatever it is I am not interested right now. I kind of get the feeling that maybe I should find my own place or at least a place not Mikael's to live. Soon. He is on a weird bend ever since he came home that first night with Jasmine.

Scarlett exits her room just as I turn the corner so I stop and wait for her to reach me, "It sounds like issues downstairs. Let's try not to be noticed as we leave."

She rolls her eyes and nods, "Agreed. I got to find a place without so much damn drama. This is not going to work for me."

"You know, I was thinking the same thing. Want to get a place together? Maybe we could get Jasmine in on it too. Have our own little bachelor pad."

Scarlett tips her head to one side, "That isn't the worst idea you ever had. Maybe we check in with her after the club tonight?"

I nod, we are on the landing and I put my finger to my lips and then point toward Mikael's office. I know she can hear him too, but we tune so many things out that she may not have noticed it. We step quietly on our way down, about halfway Mikael's mutterings grow suddenly louder and we freeze.

"...and why would she say it like that? Is that her plan? Maybe she wants to destroy my way of life. Or maybe she is already halfway to choosing Leonidas. What if she does choose him? I can't let it stand. I can't. She just has to choose me."

I look at Scarlett to find her shaking her head in disgust. I nod and we get moving again. Still quieter than mice as we pick up the pace to get out before anyone sees us.

Outside we pick up the pace with less concern about noise. Not smelling anyone near we clear the fence in a leap and hit the ground running. Our plans for tonight are changing.

Once we get a mile or so away from the house we slow to a walk. Scarlett looks at me, "What the hell was that?"

I shrug, "The reason why we are going to move out very soon? I mean, he just keeps getting weirder and I don't know what is going on with him. I'm not sure I want to. For now, maybe we should just go visit a club, have a quick feed and go find Jasmine. I think maybe she needs the warning. They just went out last night, I think."

She nods, "And we start the house hunt when we get home. Maybe we can find something with a little less old white guy personality than Morhall has."

"I like it. Oh look, there's Club Five." She grins at me as we angle across the parking lot toward the doors for a little bite.

Inside we wander over to the bar and order drinks while we wait. Scarlett nudges me as the bartender sets our drinks on the bar. I turn and follow her gaze, I see the group she is watching. They look like the kind of guys that we want to take a bite out of, and they are looking at us. How convenient. Scarlett starts things by smiling at them. One of them saunters over, "Hello ladies, we couldn't help but notice you noticing us. Would you like to come party with us?" He puts a slight emphasis on the word party and we smile pretty for the man. Cooing at him and telling him how strong he looks, but we aren't sure that we should. We let him talk us into coming over. Drinks in hand we sit at the table with them. One guy looks really upset and he stands, "Ladies, it is very nice to meet you. I am leaving and I suggest you do the same," he glares at the other men, "for your own safety."

He turns and walks away, Scarlett catches my eye with a grin, she knows how to pick them.

Twenty minutes later we go visit the ladies room, careful to leave our drinks on the table with them. We've played out this scene a hundred times and it is always the same. They always drug our drinks while we visit the bathroom, and they are always surprised in the alley when we are suddenly not affected.

Returning from the bathroom we find the men laughing, near giggling, at something. When we innocently ask, "What's so funny?"

The guys laugh harder and one of them says, "Milton over here choked and some of his drink came flying out his nose."

They laugh and propose a toast to Milton, for being tonight's entertainment. We laugh too and sip our drinks. We can taste the drugs they added but we just go along with the show. A few minutes later I say, "Oh, I don't feel so great." Scarlett ducks her head to keep her smile from being noticed, "I think I need to go home Scar, are you ready to leave?"

She nods, faking for all she's worth, "Yeah, I don't feel so great either."

We stand and the guys stand with us, making excuses about making sure we get to our car all right. Outside we stumble a little and they quickly grab our arms and drag us off to the alley. In the dark alley we wait for them to pick the spot they feel is less likely to be seen. As soon as they stop walking and start getting handsy we stand. Only one suddenly looks as scared as they all should be. He turns to run but Scarlett is fast, her arm shoots out to grab him and drag him in close to her body. "Where are you going Steve?" She purrs into his ear, "Don't you want to party?"

Steve begins to struggle in earnest then. Milton tries to help him and Scarlett grabs him by the throat saying, "So eager! I love it." She sinks her fangs into Steve's neck and drinks deeply. Steve stops struggling and leans into it because nothing feels better than the bite of a vampire.

Milton tries to escape Scarlett's hold on him while I grab the other two in a hug, "Ooh, I just love it when they struggle like this!" I squeal as I hold the two in place and biting one I begin to feed. His blood is sweet from all the liquor and I drain him quickly. Licking his neck to heal the bites I release him to turn my full attention on the other guy.

He is horrified, "Let me go, I wouldn't have done anything, I swear!"

I smile wide at him, "Oh sugar, don't lie. It makes the blood taste bad." I caress his back and slip a hand around his neck, "I'm so hungry, you don't want me to go hungry do you?"

He is caught in my eyes, the terror he feels pushed away for a moment as I bring his face down to mine and kiss his lips. He tastes of cigars and rum, not the worst flavor ever and I kiss my way along his jawline, down his neck to the sweet spot where shoulder and neck meet. He moans in pleasure as I sink my fangs into him. His hands roam my body at first, as he gets weaker they fall to hang at his sides.

His life gone I lick the wounds and drop the body. I look to Scarlett, she is surveying the alley, her two men lay on the ground at her feet. "There are a couple of dumpsters here and they smell like they are mostly full. We can dump them in those and be on our way."

I nod and we get to work. Opening the dumpster nearest us releases the most awful stench, "Yuck! We chose the right one, hurry up and let's get away from this."

We toss the bodies in as quietly as we can and close the

lid. There is a fence at the back of the alley and rather than be seen leaving the alley we head for that. We peep over the top edge of the fence, this place is backed up to trees. Excellent. Hopping over we start a brisk walk through the wooded copse to find the other side and get ourselves to Jasmine's place, now that we have eaten.

* * *

Twenty minutes later we arrive at Jasmine's empty trailer. Well shit. I look back down the driveway, "She's probably at work. Let's go there. It should be fun, plus we can see the show."

Scarlett says, "Yeah, I could use a drink anyway. Those guys were a little too bland, I need something to wash away the taste."

I laugh as we head for Club Amnesia. Walking up to the door the guy checking id's tells us, "Auditions are Wednesdays, noon to three."

We giggle, "No sugar, we aren't here to audition. We need to see our friend Jasmine."

He raises an eyebrow, "You here to cause trouble?"

Scarlett says, "Nope. No drama, just personal business."

"Hmmpph. Stay there." He opens the door and leans in, returning to his seat he continues to watch us. It's adorable. He is a big guy, I'm sure he thinks he could just throw us if we caused a problem.

Someone opens the door from inside, "Whatcha need big man?"

He turns to look at the guy, "These two," turning back he says, "what are your names?"

I wave at the new guy with a grin, "This is Scarlett and I am Chloe."

Big guy frowns, "Scarlett and Chloe want to see Jasmine. Go see if she is free. Report back if she isn't, don't leave me hanging like last time jackass."

The guy laughs and waves at us as he slips away from the door. The doorman stares menacingly at us and it is just giving me the urge to toy with him. "So, is this your day job or do you do something else?"

He grunts, "I craft doilies for bikinis. Want to model for me?"

Scarlett laughs and before I can reply Jasmine is at the door beckoning us in. I tell door guy, "We can talk about modeling things later sweet cheeks."

"Hmmph." Is the last thing I hear from him as the door closes behind us.

Jasmine takes us to a table and a woman comes by for a drink order. She leaves and we start to tell her what we overheard earlier when some guy stumbles over to our table and leans in really close saying, "Hey there Amber! Can I get a dance from—" He cuts off when a bouncer grabs him and bodily hauls him out the door.

She shrugs and we carry on. She looks concerned as she tells us, "The other night he said he had a dream about the world ending if I didn't pick him. No wait, he said his world. I get the impression that the two are not the same."

Scarlett laughs, "You know they aren't. That man has never been anything but rich, male, and pale. His world is different than any of ours has ever been. I mean, I understand why he would fear the loss of his world."

Jasmine laughs with us but she has a pinched look to

her eyes. I wonder what else is going on that this only added to? "Jasmine, we were talking tonight about getting our own place. Morhall is feeling less and less like a place that we want to be. Would you want to join us?"

Her eyes go round and her mouth drops open, "Really?"

"Yes really. I mean, you can think about it if you want or need to but you would be a good addition to our women's club. Even if you are currently seeing a couple of guys that are possibly pretty fucking problematic." I chuckle, "It is highly likely that we will date our own problematic people in the future, we definitely have in the past."

She laughs, "Ok. I was thinking I needed to get a different place anyway and I think it would be fun living in a bachelor pad. Keep me on the single life like I need to be. How are we going to do this? Are we going to go online shopping? How do we house hunt at night?"

Scarlett laughs, "No. I have a lady, she does real estate. She doesn't care that I can only meet her at night, she likes the color of my money."

A guy comes up to the table then, saying, "Hey Amber, you going to make your set? You're on in twenty."

"Shit. Yes. Be right there." She turns to us, "I got to go. Let me know what I need to contribute. I want my own bathroom. I, uh, money isn't an issue now. So I want to pay an equal share."

She starts to leave, turns around and hugs us, leaning across the table. A couple guys whistle and she is grinning as she releases us. She walks away without another look and we finish our drinks. I flag the woman that brought us the drinks so I can pay for them. When I ask her what the charge is she says that Amber got it for us. So we each grab some cash and tip her well before we leave.

On the way out the doorman stops us, "Ladies, would you like an escort to your car? There are some gentlemen loitering just the edge of the lot that you probably wouldn't be safe meeting in the dark alone."

We laugh and I pat his shoulder, "Thanks for the warning. We are the things that go bump in the night, they should be afraid. Which way are they? I'm feeling... fun tonight."

He cocks his head to one side and smiles at me, "Ok. Enjoy." He points off to a darker area and I can just see the three guys leaned against the wall.

Scarlett grins at me and we walk that way. I stop a few steps away and turn, "Don't hear anything for the next few minutes, you're cute and I would hate to have to kill you."

He freezes for a moment before he nods in agreement, facing himself away from the dark area.

I catch up with Scarlett in an instant. As we draw close to them they start to whisper to each other, giggling like the little idiots they are. We walk past them, they try to stop us but we just keep walking. They follow us into the even darker part of the alley, the fools. Only men would follow someone into a dark alley like this after being unable to stop their progress with the thought that somehow this is going to turn out well for them.

The alley stinks, I think the places flanking this are in the food business or possibly the dead people business. Whatever it is, the smell makes me want to gag. We stop and the men try to yank us about but we turn to face them as we please. They are running their mouthes about what they are going to do to stupid bitches like us. I tell Scarlett, "I'm still full from earlier. I don't thinkI could eat another one."

"Me too. Maybe we should just kick their asses and stuff them in the dumpster. Scrubbing that stench off should teach them something."

"I like it. You want two or one?"

"One, I'm tired and I still have to contact my person."

"I hoped you would say that!"

$$Twenty$$

JASMINE

I'M UPSIDE DOWN on the pole when he sits at the front of the stage. Leonidas. His name echoes through my body. I haven't seen him since our date. I still haven't gotten his number or a replacement phone, but he said he had some business to take care of and he didn't know how long it would be. It doesn't matter. He isn't mine. I sure would like to give him a ride, anyway.

My moves on stage grow more seductive now that he is watching. I can feel myself getting hotter and more into it. The money is stacking up around the stage. Out of the corner of my eye, I see Leonidas has made a stack for me as well. I finish my song on my knees at the front of the stage, running a hand up my body slowly.

The guys sitting around the stage are howling, calling my name and begging me to be theirs. I strut the stage, slowly collecting the money while Leonidas smirks at me. I pick up the money in front of him, raise an eyebrow in challenge, and he just grins.

Moments after I get back to the dressing room, one of the women serving drinks comes in to tell me a guy has requested a private dance. I ask her where he is sitting, she tells me, "Near the front of the stage, to the left. Tall, dark, and a voice made to entice."

I nod, laughing. "I'll be with him shortly. Thanks!" I change outfits, slipping on a black thong with matching star pasties and a zip front mini skirt with matching zip front crop tank. To finish the outfit, I slip on platform, spike-heeled, thigh-high boots.

Stepping out of the back room, I nearly run into the bouncer waiting for me. He points at Leonidas and says, "Sue said he is getting a dance?" At my nod, he says, "Give me five to get your room set up. You going to tell him the rules?"

I laugh, "Oh yes, I am." Bill chuckles and heads for the room while I walk over to the table Leonidas is sitting at. "So, I'm told you would like a private dance?"

He looks me up and down, a slow smile spreading across his face, saying, "Oh yeah. I definitely want a dance from you." He nudges a chair out for me. "Have a seat."

I pull the chair away from the table and I sit. "I have to tell you the rules. We have new rules that only apply to certain dancers and I get to be one of them." He raises a brow at me and I continue, "We have a reclined chair that you will sit in. Your hands can be tied or cuffed, but they have to be secured behind you. Your hips must be secured to the chair as well. If you thrash about, the dance ends and you don't get a refund for the time left. No touching. If you work at touching me, the dance will end. Lastly, Bill will be there watching you."

"You know they don't have anything that could hold me if I didn't choose to be held?"

"I do. But if you don't play along with it, you get no dance. You want a different dance, talk to me after work. You going to behave, or should I tell Bill not to worry about getting the room set up?"

"I'll behave. I'm eager to see just why they lock your people down. Do you pay the guy off when you feed?"

"We can talk about that some other time. Bill is on his way over. The room is ready."

Bill steps up to the table, saying, "Hi. I'm Bill. I'll be your monitor for the dance. Has Amber explained the procedure?"

Leonidas looks at me, "Yes... Amber has explained it quite thoroughly."

Bill claps his hands together. "Great. Let's go." He leads Leonidas and me to the room. Moving to stand by the chair, he asks Leonidas, "Would you prefer cuffs or rope?"

"Rope, thanks." He lies on the chair and Bill kneels behind it and ties his hands. That done, he stands and moves to Leonidas' hips and picks up the seat belt straps hanging from either side, fastening them over him before pulling the strap snug across him. Bill walks to the light, switches and dims the lighting, hitting the button to start a sultry song with a good drum beat and really nice bass.

I walk over to the foot of the chair, saying, "Ready?"

He nods, and Bill hits his timer. I trail a hand in the air, just a scant inch from touching him as I walk slowly to be even with his hips. He sucks in a breath as I lean over him, carefully gripping the opposite edge of the chair and swinging my leg over him so I stand straddling the chair. Straightening, I undulate with the music, running my hands over my body. Reaching my breasts, I slide my hand across to the zipper. Grasping the tab with thumb and forefinger, I lean in close to him, using my other hand to brace myself on the edge of the chair. His eyes focus on my cleavage as I pull the zipper down till I free my breasts from the restraint. I lean forward slightly before I swing back to stand upright. I rotate my hips over him as I slip the top down my arms and toss it off to the side.

I spend some time moving with the music over him, lowering myself over him till nothing but air and opportunity separate us before I straighten to run my hands down my body from the top of my breasts over my belly and down to the bottom hem of my skirt. Leonidas' breath is rapid as he focuses on the fingers pulling the zipper up incrementally. I reach the top and toss the skirt off to one side.

Grinding over him as he watches the thin fabric of my thong dip and sway over his jeans encased hardness. I run my hands back up my body to cup my breasts as I undulate over him and he groans.

I hear Bill's timer chiming, and I realize why he is groaning. I smile down at him as Bill turns up the lights, asking, "Was it good for you?"

He slants me a fiery look. "You know it was."

Bill chuckles as I swing my leg over and gather up my clothing, "Great, isn't she? Guess you know why the precautions now." He kneels down and unties Leonidas' hands. Standing up, he says, "I'll let you unbuckle the hip strap."

I finish zipping my clothes on and give them a wave, saying, "I have to go finish my last set." Strolling back to the dressing room, I have a grin plastered on my face and an extra sway in my hips. I always feel extra after a private dance and it is even better this time since it was him.

I finish my set and get cashed out. Changing into street clothes, I head for the back door. Bill is waiting there, and he says, "Your last lap dance guy is outside. You need me to walk you home?"

I grin and tell him, "Oh honey, I'm more dangerous than anything waiting for me out there in the dark."

He chuckles, "Well, I guess you are at that. See ya."

I step outside and I take a deep breath. I smell a trace of Mikael, like he came through checking on me. Mostly I smell Leonidas standing across the parking lot. I walk over to him, looking up at him. I ask, "How's things?" as I flick my eyes to his zipper and back up to his eyes.

He chuckles, low and deep, sending gooseflesh racing across my body, "Uncomfortable. Care to help me ease some tension?"

I laugh, saying, "I would love to help you alleviate some tension."

* * *

Mikael

I watch her meet up with him. She smiles at him and I can smell her arousal from the roof I stand on. I hate him. I want to hate her, but I can't. She is my love, my wife. The reason I am cursed to this existence.

She is mine, even if she doesn't want to admit it. I watch them walk off into the night. Her with her hands on her backpack straps and him with hands in pockets. What can she possibly see in his work boot and jeans wearing scruffiness?

He can't give her the life of a princess the way I can. Why bother with him?

Wait, that's it! She is using him to make me jealous! I slip my hands into the pockets of my slacks. She could be working to make me jealous, but I can't take the chance that she might choose him.

It may be time to take some actions to ensure he is out of the way for a time. Perhaps a baited trap that gets him locked up? Or maybe a shipment that suddenly goes astray. Yes. He'll go handle that himself and if I get the right people working on it, I could have him chasing them for days before they let him have the supply.

Making sure no one is watching, I hop off the roof and land lightly in the alley. I think I will swing by her place, see if he stayed. If he didn't, perhaps I will offer to take her out hunting.

I get as far as the park driveway when I feel her pleasure begin. Quickly turning around and walking the other way, I shut out all her feelings. I just can't allow her emotions to flow through me as she cums for him.

The walk home is fast and I slip into the house, heading straight for my office and the liquor stores I keep in there. I pull a fresh bottle of brandy from the cabinet and grabbing a rocks glass I move to sit at my desk. Pouring a large shot, I down it in one go. I can still feel her coming. I pour another shot and adjust myself. The pressure is painful. Shooting the brandy, I lean back in the chair. I pour a full glass, this time to sip. The brandy dulls the emotions coming through the bond and I sigh in relief. My cock finally begins to relax as I make it through half the glass. Perhaps I will be able to sleep today if she finishes, and I have had enough to drink. I slam down the rest of the glass and pour another. Standing up, I only wobble a little as I grab the bottle and head upstairs, sipping from the glass as I go.

Turning her in a moment of passion may be the single dumbest thing I have ever done, but, gods, she presses all my buttons. Having sex with her was the best I have had in a century, or more at least. Angry fucking her made it hotter, though the consequences were pretty dire. I wasn't sure she would make it for a little bit and then she did and suddenly I have a whole new set of problems as my sweet wife turns into this demanding woman with the morals of a sailor in port.

I knock back the rest of the glass as I see the sun coming up through a crack in the curtains of my bedroom. Setting the bottle and cup on my nightstand, I wrestle with buttons and finally manage to remove my clothing. Slipping between the sheets is bliss, and I close my eyes. Jasmine is nothing more than a faint scent left in the room as I drift off to sleep.

Twenty-One

MIKAEL

I WAIT for her the next night, just down the block from Club Amnesia. It seems like an eternity before she leaves the club and draws near to me. I watch her scent the air as she walks and I see her eyes zero in on me. I step out of the shadows and she smiles at me, "You trying to sneak up on me Mikael? All laying in wait like some murderer or something."

I laugh and slip my arm around her waist as she comes even with me. Walking next to her, I say, "I missed you. I wanted to see you again. I haven't seen you since our date."

She is silent a minute before saying, "Yeah... I... You have been pushing how you want things to be pretty hard. I'm just not comfortable with it. I'm, I think maybe we should take a break from seeing each other for a while. So we can sort ourselves. I need to get my head straight and I think you do, too. What do you think?"

My mind races as she speaks. She is going to choose

him, I just know it. Now she wants time apart to sort ourselves. I know what she plans! Think Mikael, how can I turn this to my advantage? "Maybe you are right. I think some time apart could clear my head. I have been a little much, haven't I?" She smiles, relief plain on her face. Perfect. I stop us and tug her close to me, wrapping my arms around her and looking down at her, saying, "Before we go off to our separate corners, how would you feel about making love one more time? To tide me over till you and I are ready to see each other again?"

She smiles a soft little smile, "I don't know. I mean, will you promise me that you will go home in the morning? Can you do that? I don't want to hurt you by letting you get closer when I am trying to get some space. Are you going to be okay?"

Giving her a squeeze, I tell her, "I have waited lifetimes for you. Now you are here and you need some time. I can do anything knowing you are going to be part of my life again."

She hugs me back, laying her head on my chest. I smile, knowing I have her fooled. She releases me and I school my face to the appropriate expression, softening my eyes and putting on a dopey smile. She takes my hand and we walk to her trailer. Next time she comes back I will make sure that she does not get turned, can't have her remembering things like this. The things she remembers are incredibly annoying.

We arrive at her trailer and I ask her, "Why haven't you found a different place yet?"

She shrugs, "I've been busy. I haven't had time to do anything about it."

I look at her, saying, "You barely need sleep and you are immune to the effects of the sun. What's the real reason?"

She turns away, crossing her arms in front of her as she gazes out the window. "I... This is the first place I have had to myself. I've just really loved it and I am loath to leave it, even for something better."

I cross the room in an instant, wrapping my arms around her from behind, saying, "I'm sorry, love. I will say this, you could go ahead and buy a place. Just let it sit and wait for you to be ready. That way you'll have it. Or at least monitor the market in case something you love comes up."

She nods, "I'll think about it."

Jasmine

I turn around in the circle of Mikael's arms and we kiss. He is being very agreeable, and I am not sure what to make of it beyond suspicion. But I am suspicious of most people, so I don't know that it actually means anything.

He lifts me, and I wrap my legs around his waist as he walks to the bedroom. We make love and it is good, but I feel like something is off or missing. I'm on edge and I don't know why.

He is lying with his head on my chest, fingers idly drawing circles on my hip when he says, "Are you set on us taking a break? You're sure it's what you want to do?"

Sighing, I say, "It isn't what I want to do, Mikael. It is necessary until you can learn to respect my boundaries. You don't own me and I will not be your possession."

He sits up and gets off the bed, fishing his pants from off the floor. He slips his shirt on, leaving it hanging open. I sit up and look around for something to throw on. I see Mikael moving out of the corner of my eye, but I think nothing of it till I am slammed back on the bed, pain exploding in the right side of my chest. My eyes open again to see Mikael over me, his face contorted in a way I have never seen. He twists the knife and I scream. My eyes screwed shut as I reach for the power deep inside of me. I get to that core and the power is straining, pushing, trying to get out. I just open the door and let it go. The reverberations of whatever my magic did that caused Mikael to fly off of me are still vibrating through the room. His weight gone, I sit up and feel the tug of muscles and skin trying to knit up around the knife. I look away as I grasp the handle and rip it out before I lose my nerve, teeth gritted, trying not to scream again as I snatch the knife from my body and throw it at the wall.

I can see Mikael laying on the ground outside. He hit a tree. Pretty hard if the condition of the tree is anything to go by. I throw on a shirt and pants, cursing every time the still healing wound twinges. Blade twisting bastard.

Jumping lightly to the ground through the giant hole in my bedroom wall, I realize I definitely need to move now. I stalk over to Mikael, who is twitching as his spinal cord heals. Looking around for witnesses and seeing none, I snatch him up by the shoulders and sink my teeth into his neck. I drink deep and I bite down hard, making sure he isn't enjoying this. When I have drunk my fill, he is withered. The healing has stopped or slowed dramatically for now. I walk back to the trailer, holding him out at arm's length. "You son of a motherfucker. How dare you?" I toss him on my bed while I slip on some shoes. "You couldn't just give me some space, could you? Noooo. You were all mad because your possession was out of pocket. Had to go trying to kill me. Fucker."

I look at my now bloodstained coverlet, and I want to kick the crap out of him. Instead, I roll him up in the damn thing so the bloodstains aren't showing. I grab my backpack and throw him over my shoulder. "Sure is nice how quiet you are right now." I say as I head toward his place. "I guess that since I have you as a captive audience, I can tell you some things. You are an insufferable ass. Your high handed attitude had me wishing I could leave you back then, but it wasn't an option. I remembered everything Mikael. Like the fact that you went after me because I was part of the royal family. You were just a greedy son of a bitch. The only reason you had anything was that you married into it and then your wife died in childbirth. Oddly enough, your child died with the nanny days later." I give him a shake. "But you surely wouldn't know anything about that, would you, Mikael?" I have made it to the gate. It is early morning. The sun will come up soon. Looking around and scenting the air, I am sure no one is about as I hop the fence and take my burden to the front door. Opening it, I walk in and shout, "Hello! A little help here!"

Everyone runs into the entry and stops eyeing my pink, ruffled coverlet. I set Mikael down and grab an edge. One swift yank and he rolls out; looking a bit like a desiccated corpse. I hear gasps all around and Scarlett says, "Oh Jasmine, are you all right?"

"I am, no thanks to this asshole. He tried to kill me, but thankfully his grasp of the anatomy of the body is poor and he stabbed me in the right side of my chest." They all gasp and look at me. A shift of the collar of my shirt to one side lets them see the dried blood. "I don't want to kill him. I loved him once. But," I look at Chloe and Scarlett, "I am going to move to a more secure location. It would be great if you could just let him heal as slowly as possible. If he comes after me like this again…" I sigh, "I don't know what I will do." My shoulders slump because the thought of killing him hurts my heart. Even if he tried to kill me just a little while ago. He is the oldest part of my history. From my first lifetime here on earth. He was someone I loved once, even when I knew he was using me. I think he loved me. Maybe in some strange way he still does. "I have to go explain the missing wall to the property manager now. Chloe, could I talk to you outside a moment?"

She walks out with me, shutting the door behind us. I hand her my phone and raise my brows at her. She enters her number and hits send, then lets her phone ring and then hangs up, handing it back to me. She grabs me in a fierce hug. Then she releases me, opening the door as she walks inside. I shrug an arm out of my backpack and bring it around front to open it and take out my sunglasses. The sun will be up before I get home if I don't hurry and I have no hurry in me for going to deal with this.

Twenty-Two

JASMINE

I GET BACK to the park, and the manager is sitting on his porch having a smoke. I walk over and tell him about the wall with promises to pay for the repairs. He laughs, "S'all good. Shit happens. I'll send my guy over today and let you know what he charges me. Should have seen it the night the back place tried to kill each other. The whole inside was destroyed. You only got one wall and you are going to pay for it without me having to badger you. We're good."

"Thank you, I really feel bad about this wall. And I am going to move soon. Getting a house with roommates, safety in numbers, right?"

He nods, "Yeah, yeah. I get that. Be sad to see you go."

I say, "Thanks again," before I turn to leave. As I step around the end of the trailer, a breeze wafts the scent of Leonidas to me. I breathe deeply. He smells so good. I make it to the trailer as the sun crests the horizon, and I see Leonidas standing in the yard, looking at the missing wall.

I watch him unconcerned with the sun and I know I have passed on the ability to walk in the sun to him. What else did I pass on to him? I can only hope that he doesn't go fucking things up now that he can day walk. I don't want to think about what the consequences for that would be. Walking over, I stand next to him. He glances at me, asking, "Do I want to know how you managed to blow out an entire wall?"

"No."

He eyes me, asking, "Is it something I probably should know?"

Sigh. "Yes. I doubt he will stop at me."

"He? Ah, Mikael. What did he do?"

I feel stupid tears burning the backs of my eyes and I turn my face away, "He tried to kill me."

I can feel the anger rolling off of Leonidas but his hands are gentle as he turns me to face him. A fat tear rolls down from my traitorous eyes as he says, "Are you ok? I know you are still alive, but are you ok?"

I wipe away the tear, saying, "Yes, I am as good as I can be. A little upset, but I think that is reasonable even if I don't appreciate it."

He kisses my forehead and takes me in his arms. I press my face into his neck and just stand there, accepting the comfort of a man that doesn't want me dead right now. He releases me after a time and with his hands on my shoulders he looks me in the eye, "Now where is Mikael?"

I can see the murder in his eyes and my heart leaps for it. "He is recovering. I don't want you to kill him."

His eyes narrow, "Recovering?"

"I might have blasted him out of the trailer and into the tree there," I point behind him to the tree that, while standing, has definitely seen better days. "It injured his spine enough that he could not get right back up. I drained him to the point of death if he had been human. Then I rolled him up in a blanket and took him to his home."

"So he is home? Good."

"Leonidas, I mean it. I don't want him dead."

He shouts in frustration, "Why the hell not? He tried to kill you!"

I look down, saying, "He is the only link to the first time I was on this planet. He has been a part of every life I have lived since then. I loved him. I don't want him dead."

Leonidas paces, stomping and cursing. "Damn it, woman. For fuck — Son of a dirty cracker!" He stops and looks at me, grinding out, "You don't want him dead. Why does he want you dead?"

"He met me when I got off work and he has pressured me a lot lately. I told him we needed some time apart so he could learn to respect my boundaries. He seemed agreeable, asked if we could have sex one last time. I thought nothing of it. After, well, he asked if a break was definitely what I wanted. I told him it was and as I was looking for a shirt to throw on, he stabbed me. Then he twisted the knife, and I let loose my powers. He wants me dead because he can't own me. Because I refused to be his possession." Hot, angry tears stream down my face and I can't even care right now. "I just don't understand the need to own someone."

Leonidas nods, "Wait." He pinches the bridge of his nose and closes his eyes for a moment, saying, "I need to make sure I understand. He showed up at your work as you were leaving. You two are walking and talking. You tell him that the two of you need time apart. He is ok and wants to fuck one more time. You agree, the two of you have sex. Afterward, he asks if you definitely want a break and when you affirm that, he stabs you. I have the general gist of things?"

I nod and he shouts, "Then why won't you let me take care of that bastard for you?" Raw power rolls off of Leonidas, but I feel no fear. Mild curiosity in the back of my mind, but I shove it away for another time. He takes a few pacing laps in front of me, mumbling and cursing. He stops in front of me and runs a hand through his hair, leaving it mussed and the tie he had holding it in place falling broken to the ground. "Ok. Ok. I know it is your choice and as much as I would like to pressure you about getting rid of an enemy that will surely come for you again, I won't."

"Thank you." My phone rings and I pull it out to look at it, seeing it is Chloe I tell Leonidas, "I need to take this." He nods and goes back to pacing as I answer, "Hi Chloe, got any good news?"

"No. Yes. Yes, and no. First, you need to get all your money transferred right now. He plans to close out the account. Second, we scored a vacation place for temporary digs. I'll text you the address. Get your ass there tonight. You do not want to be where you are tonight. Promise me you will come?"

Chloe sounds on the verge of tears, and I tell her, "I promise! I will be there. And I moved the money already. I just opened a new account and had the original bank transfer it all into that account. There is maybe a hundred left in there? I am slowly transferring it to the account I had before all this started. I started getting a weird feeling I needed to and I listen to my gut."

I hear her take a shuddering breath. She says, "Good. Good. Watch your back. Don't let anyone you don't know get close to you. Scarlett and I will see you tonight." I hear my phone ding and she says, "I just sent you the address to the place. Scarlett and I will be there shortly after sunset. You need to leave your place the minute you wake up. And ditch your phone. He has a tracker in it. He knows you are at the trailer now."

"Motherfucker. All right. I'll see you tonight. You two are ok, right? He isn't after you or anything?"

"No. He does not know we are leaving. He thinks we will help him. But he also called some other guys. They are supposed to come see you tonight. I don't think he trusts any of us that far. Sebastian, Eason, Asher, and Quinn all are leaving tonight too. They found their own place."

"Ok, I got to go. I am handling some things right now, but I will see you tonight."

"Be careful." Chloe says before hitting the button to end the call.

Stuffing my phone into my back pocket, I find Leonidas has stopped pacing and is watching me. I shrug, saying, "He is sending people here tonight. I gotta pack. Maybe I'll call a mover to put my bed in storage."

Leonidas pulls out his phone and taps it a few times before putting it to his ear. Someone on the other end answers and he says, "Send a box truck and some guys to the address I am sending you. They need to bring boxes and pack this place up, put it in storage. Send a new phone with them." He ends the call and taps out a message before shoving his phone back in his pocket. "The downside to having conversations around vampires is that nothing is private. I heard what she said and dammit, you are going to let me help you. You won't let me kill him. I could only wish it was because you were going to do it. I would pay to see that. But no. So you get to let me help. You will have a new phone through my company plan. We don't install trackers, ever. If you insist on paying for it, send the check to Knight Construction. My guys are going to be here soon. All you need to pack is bags for until you can take delivery of your things. I will have your number and I will be calling you. If you get into trouble and don't call me again, I am going to yell at you. I might spank you too."

I chuckle, asking, "Are we still talking about punishment?"

He narrows his eyes at me. "Yes."

With a sigh, I sit on the ground. He comes to sit beside me. I look over at him, "Thank you. I appreciate your restraint and your aid. Even if I didn't ask for the help."

He just nods and bumps my shoulder with his. I remember he said Knight Construction and I look at him, "Why did you name your company Knight Construction?"

He shrugs, saying, "It's my last name. Seemed like a good idea. Um, the guys are not exactly human, so they might be a little surprised to see us in the sun. Do you want to go inside or let the cat out of the bag? They know what I am, one whiff of you and they will know you are the same."

"One whiff? What are they? Dogs?"

Leonidas chuckles, "I don't think they like being called that but, it is pretty close."

"Get out! You have werewolves working for you?"

"They aren't all wolves, but yes. It solves a lot of problems when we work together, especially the daylight thing. That isn't an issue now, thank you. You know, if anything, I owe you for this. I have seen the sun rise and set every day this week. I don't know how to repay you for that."

"I think you made a lot of headway already, even though it was an accident of sorts. I didn't intend to do that. Being bitten during sex is just about my favorite thing." As I grin at him, his answering grin makes lots of my parts wake right up. I stand, "Guess I need to pack. Go ahead and let the cat out of the bag. I don't know what will come of it. Other vampires might not appreciate it."

He nods and stands. "I'll wait here while you pack. The guys should be here soon."

I jump into the trailer and look around. It's a shitty trailer, but damned if I won't miss it. I sigh. Better get started. It takes me a lot less time than I thought it would to pack up what I need for a week. Most of my dance clothing is in my locker at work and the rest of my clothes are what I ordered when I first arrived at Mikael's place. I put it all into a bag and toss my toiletries into a plastic bag before throwing them in on top. Grabbing that and my backpack, I'm ready to go. Luckily, I am all out of blood, so no worries about that. Just as I get to the opening in the wall, a large truck pulls into the driveway. They look surprised to see Leonidas standing there, and they quickly jump out of the truck to speak to him. I listen as he gives them a short version of the story and also jerks a thumb toward me as he tells them that I am the one it came from. They accept it and make jokes. Leonidas warns them it would be better if this stayed quiet, as no one knew what the rest of the vampire community would think or do about this development. The guys nod and the leader says, "Where do we start?"

I speak then, "In here. Mostly, it is just a bed. But I really love this bed, even if my blood is all over it now. Just take the bed. I never bothered getting anything else. Oh! And the books! Bring the books."

The guys nod and the lead tells one to get the tools out of the truck along with the phone. He jumps past me into the room, nearly hitting the bed. I hear him inhale, "Holy shit. You were stabbed, weren't you? I thought you meant... well, something else. Also, you smell damn good. Go stand somewhere else while we work before you end up with a proper fuck."

My lips pull up on one side and I say, "Sure thing, wolf man." As I jump out on the ground. I hear him growling behind me and I giggle as I walk over to Leonidas.

He is shaking his head, saying, "Don't antagonize the wolves." But he is smiling, so I am not concerned. Suddenly serious, he says, "Where did you plan to stay today?"

Shrugging, I tell him, "I haven't got that far. Why?"

He looks away and then back at me. Watching my face, he says, "What would you say if I invited you to sleep at my place until you are ready to go meet your friends tonight?"

With a grin, I say, "You want to sleep with me? Leonidas, you're so forward today! I would really appreciate that."

He sighs in relief, saying, "Good. I wasn't sure how I

was going to convince you if you didn't like the idea. It is the safest place I can think of for you right now. If you like, I can even drop you off at the new place tonight. Here is your new phone."

He passes me a phone and I just stare at it for a moment before I take it from him. Opening the other phone, I pull up the message Chloe sent me and I take a picture. Resetting the phone to erase everything, I toss it under the trailer. I look back at Leonidas, saying, "Ready to take me to bed?"

* * *

Did you love this book?
Does early access get you excited?
Find my early access subscription at Ream Stories.

About the Author

Rhiannon writes steamy paranormal romance. She is an avid reader of many authors in a variety of genre though she tends more toward paranormal.

She has three former pound puppies that she dotes on and three daughters that she adores.

Rhiannon has lived in multiple states though she is currently residing in North Carolina. Wandering, witching, and reading with her puppies and husband are what she does when she isn't writing.

To learn about what is happening in Rhiannon's world and get loads of pupper cuteness, sign up for the by using the QR code below to visit my website.

Also by Rhiannon Futch

Get early access to whatever I am writing now by subscribing

at Ream Stories

The Daughter of the Moon series-

Selena Rose, Daughter of the Moon Book 1

Thorns of the Rose, Daughter of the Moon Book 2

Heart of the Rose, Daughter of the Moon Book 3

The Fate's Chronicles series

A Vampire's Fate

A Vampire's Treasure

A Vampire's Dream

A Vampire's Chase

A Vampire's Fight

Fated for Halloween - only available via email signup

The Belancore Witches of North Carolina series

Witchy Ever After

A Witchy New Year

My Witchy Valentine

Sin series

Sin on a Dark Knight

Sin on a Broken Heart

Sin on a Burning Heart

Sin on a Vengeful Heart

The Vampire Kings Series

Mercy of the Vampire King

Shame of the Vampire King

Pursuit of the Vampire King

Prey of the Vampire King

Reign of the Vampire King

Coming soon!

Love and Vampires Series

Olivia's Fall

Olivia's Prison

Olivia's Flight

Olivia's Family

Warriors of the Old Gods series

A Dream of Blood

A Dream of Wolves

A Dream of Stone

A Dream of Ravens

A Dream of Bones